Knight Kyle

Kyle

AND
THE

Magic
Silver
Lance

Adventures Beyond
Dragon Mountain

Oliver Pötzsch

Translated by Lee Chadeayne

amazoncrossing

Text copyright © 2014 Thienemann-Esslinger Verlag GmbH, Stuttgart
By Oliver Pötzsch
Translation copyright © 2016 Lee Chadeayne
Illustrations by Sibylle Hammer
All rights reserved.

Previously published as *Ritter Kyle Kettenstrumpf* by Thienemann-Esslinger Verlag GmbH, Stuttgart, Germany, in 2014. Translated from German by Lee Chadeayne. First published in English by AmazonCrossing in 2016.

Published by AmazonCrossing, Seattle

www.apub.com

Amazon, the Amazon logo, and AmazonCrossing are trademarks of Amazon.com, Inc., or its affiliates.

ISBN-13 (Hardcover): 9781503936300
ISBN-10 (Hardcover): 1503936309
ISBN 13 (Paperback): 9781503934931
ISBN 10 (Paperback): 1503934934

Cover design by Shasti O'Leary Soudant
Illustrated by Sibylle Hammer

Printed in China

For my children, Niklas and Lily, for whom some of these tales were once intended as bedtime stories.

And for my nephews and nieces, Juri, Zeno, Rosa, Olivia, Elijana, and those yet to come, who hopefully will someday hear these stories read to them by their parents.

Table of Contents

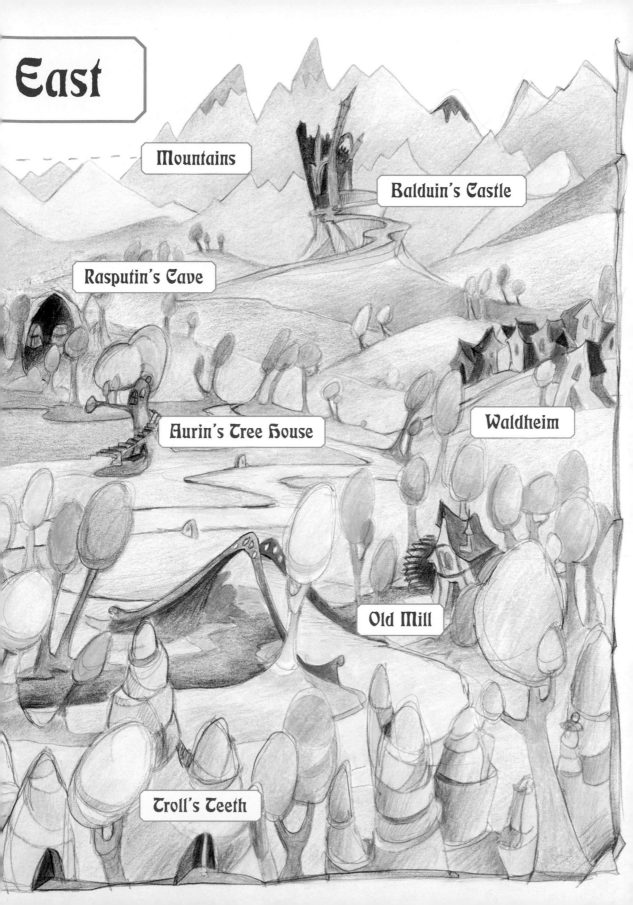

Welcome to Knight Kyle's World!

Beyond the great forest and the towering Dragon Mountain, so far away that even airplanes and rockets can't fly there, lies Fairyland. And in one corner of this land, Fairyland East, lives Knight Kyle. He has a castle with a moat, a drawbridge, and four tall towers. All around it is a forest and right through the middle of the forest a road leads to the village of Waldheim. Knight Kyle always goes there to buy sausages, cheese, raspberry soda, and best of all, lots and lots of chocolate. In Fairyland there are elves and trolls, dragons and robbers, evil magicians and bewitching damsels. And almost every day they all have the most amazing adventures . . .

Knight Kyle . . .

. . . is a fearless knight in shining armor. He loves swordplay;
he secretly loves Constance, the lady of the castle; and he loves
chocolate cookies. With his horse, Rosinante, he sets out into
the world to spread fear in the hearts of wicked men, just as his
great-grandfather Kasimir once did. A magical silver lance
had been in his family for ages and was said to render
the person wielding it invincible. The lance has been
missing for as far back as Kyle can remember,
and he is always looking for it, but so are his
worst enemies: the robber Rasputin and the
evil   magician
Balduin.

Prince Nepomuk . . .

. . . lives in the south wing of Knight Kyle's castle and has a
closet as large as all the horse stables put together. Nepomuk
likes to get all dressed up and thinks he's the most awesome
prince there ever was, but other than that he's a good fellow.
His only quarrels with Kyle are over Constance. Nepomuk
really likes Constance, but she always brushes him off. If he's
not out looking for adventure with Kyle, he's probably zoom-
ing along the castle wall on his skateboard.

Constance, the Lady of the Castle . . .

. . . is as beautiful as the morning sunrise over Dragon Mountain and as brave as a dragon. Someday she might like to marry the knight, but first he has to get over all the fighting and chasing of witches and robbers. She likes to sit on the balcony of her tower and read all kinds of books. She also makes great cookies and is friends with both the knight and the prince.

Elf Aurin . . .

. . . often helps Knight Kyle on his adventures. Aurin lives in a tree house he built himself on Willow Lake. With his bow and arrow he can hit even the tiniest knothole without even practicing, but more than anything else he likes to play his harp, which he also made himself. Unfortunately, the songs always put Kyle to sleep, and then the elf gets angry and goes back into his tree house to pout.

Balduin the Magician . . .

. . . is always scheming to get his hands on the silver lance and keeps coming up with new nasty tricks to find it and steal it. He doesn't know that Kyle himself is looking for the lance. Balduin lives in a gloomy castle up on remote Dragon Mountain with his little fire-breathing dragon, Gogol. Gogol isn't much help with his schemes, but at least he's been trained to light the candles and the stove in Balduin's kitchen.

Rasputin the Robber . . .

. . . has a shaggy beard, an eye patch, a red hat, and a rattling sword. Everyone is afraid of him. He looks grim all the time, but he's actually just very lonely. He lives in a dark cave in the forest and attacks unsuspecting travelers on the road to Waldheim. The only person he's afraid of is Knight Kyle, who once caught him and shaved off his beard. That was very embarrassing, because without a beard he didn't look scary at all.

Fairy Laureana . . .

. . . is the fairy of the forest. She takes care of the plants and animals and prepares medicine. There are many powerful spells in her old book of magic that have saved the lives of Knight Kyle and his friends. Laureana often collects her herbs in the forest, and she is the only person who knows what each one can do.

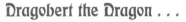

Dragobert the Dragon . . .

. . . is a ginormous dragon who lives on Dragon Mountain. Kyle once snatched Dragobert from the clutches of Balduin the magician, and ever since then Dragobert helps the knight whenever he can. His friends can ride comfortably on his back, and sometimes they fly with him to the most distant parts of Fairyland.

Arthur the Eagle . . .

. . . is known for his huge appetite for sweets. He loves to visit the knight in his castle and nibble on the cookies that Constance always has ready for him. Arthur often serves Kyle as a flying messenger. No one can fly faster or higher than he can.

The Trolls . . .

. . . are as tall as trees, as strong as giants, and as dumb as rocks, which is also what they're made of. But you have to be very careful when they are around. Woe to the traveler carrying a piece of chocolate, for trolls love chocolate even more than they love stones or sweet rock dust.

Treasure Island

One fine Sunday morning, Knight Kyle decided to do some spring-cleaning and tidy up the dark cellar in the castle. After drinking his morning cocoa, he breathed a deep sigh, then went down the stairs with a large broom and shovel.

Deeper and deeper he went, past the kitchen, the dungeon, and some dusty old wine barrels. The basement was the oldest part of the castle. Long ago it was the playground of dragons, and spiders as big as soccer balls wove their webs here. There hadn't been any dragons or spiders in the basement for a long time, but there was an awful mess. Whenever the knight didn't know where to put something, he tossed it into the basement. There were old mattresses and carriage wheels, cracked mirrors, rusty swords and suits of armor, dusty pictures of Kyle's great-grandfather Kasimir, chests with squeaky hinges, and lots more.

All morning Kyle swept, scrubbed, and polished, but he often stopped when he found an exciting book or a strange object whose purpose was a mystery to him.

Just as Kyle was about to throw a few empty soda bottles in the trash, he noticed a faded piece of paper inside one of them. Carefully he took the paper out and could hardly believe his eyes. It was an old treasure map that must have belonged to his great-grandfather. In the dark basement Kyle was barely able to make out the rough sketch and the scribbled words beneath

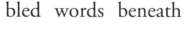

it. His heart started racing. According to the map there was a treasure chest buried on the small, uninhabited island in the middle of Willow Lake!

"Hmm, maybe the chest contains a clue to finding the silver lance," Kyle murmured. He had been looking for the magic lance as long as he could remember and had always thought his forgetful great-grandfather had lost it during one of his many adventures. A faded painting of Kasimir with the lance in his hand was stored in the armory and was all that remained of his former glory. But suppose old Kasimir had buried the lance on the island?

"I have to go right away and find out!" Kyle declared.

He mounted his horse, Rosinante, and set out on the road to Waldheim and Willow Lake, where one of his best friends, Elf Aurin, lived. Aurin had built himself a tree house in a large willow along the shore. Every evening he sat there playing lullabies on his harp for all the animals that couldn't fall asleep. When Kyle arrived, the elf was playing a melody so soothing that even the fish

closed their eyes in the middle
of the day.

"Hey, Aurin!" Kyle called,
out of breath from the long
ride. "Look what I found!"

At first, the elf was a bit

put out at being interrupted while he was playing the harp, but then he stared in amazement at the treasure map.

"If the silver lance is really hidden there, we have to go and get it right away before the robber or the magician finds it," Aurin finally whispered.

Kyle nodded grimly. He knew that his greatest adversaries were just waiting to get their hands on the lance. With it, they hoped to rule over all of Fairyland and

even tell the sun when to rise and set. He couldn't let that happen!

"No matter what's on the island, we'll get there before the villains," Kyle said firmly. They hurried down to the shore, where Aurin's sailboat was bobbing in the water. The ship was made of nothing but leaves and twigs, and two huge maple leaves that Aurin had found in a far-off forest clearing served as a sail. He'd worked hard on the rudder, weaving it from branches and reeds and had just finished it last week. Together they pushed the boat into the water and jumped in.

As soon as they got out on the lake, dark clouds appeared on the horizon, and the leaves of the trees along the shore began to rustle.

"There can't be a storm coming," Kyle muttered as he looked up at the sky, where clouds were gathering into thunderheads. The wind became stronger, the maple-leaf sail fluttered, and waves slapped against the side of the boat.

Aurin shouted, "Hang on tight!" as the storm bore down on them.

The wind was so strong that the sailboat almost disappeared between the waves, and the rain came down in buckets. Soon Kyle and Aurin couldn't even tell where the water stopped and the sky began.

"We must turn around!" Kyle shouted, trying to hold on to the wet railing, and just a moment later a wave swept over the boat and sent him flying head over heels into Willow Lake.

With his heavy armor, Kyle went down like a stone and barely had time to close his helmet. At least no water came in and he could breathe, though the air inside the helmet was sticky and smelled strongly of the cocoa, rolls, and marmalade he'd had for breakfast.

When Kyle reached the bottom, he was surprised to find he could easily stroll along the bed of the lake. It was very quiet and calm, with no sign of the storm. He trudged merrily along between carp, trout, and pike, and they all stared back at him in amazement. A little crab scampered over his toes, and now and then the knight got tangled in the seaweed that grew like giant trees down there. But each time he was able to cut himself loose with his sword.

It was only April, however, and the water was pretty cold. Soon Kyle started to shiver.

"I-I-I won't be able to stand it here m-m-much longer,"

he said, his teeth chattering, and he watched as bubbles rose to the surface from under his suit of armor. "I have to get to the island, but I can't abandon A-A-Aurin."

Kyle trembled and fretted, but finally he had an idea. He turned around and walked back a few steps until he saw the anchor rope, which had fallen from the boat, dangling down in front of him. He grabbed the rope, and step by step, foot by foot, Kyle pulled the sailboat behind him to the island in Willow Lake.

Aurin was amazed when the boat began whooshing through the waves toward the island as if pulled by a magical hand.

"Is there a sea monster down there?" he asked himself anxiously, peering over the side of the boat.

He was really worried because Kyle hadn't come back to the surface, and he didn't spot his friend again until they had almost reached the island. Like an iron walrus Kyle emerged from the water, lifted his helmet, and grinned at Aurin.

"You could have rowed a little, too," Kyle huffed. "I had to do all the work myself."

The storm was over now, and there were only a few black clouds left in the sky. Soon the two friends were able to pull the boat to safety on the shore. Unfortunately, the boat's hull had a few bad holes, and there was no way to repair it without tools.

"We'll never get off this island." The elf sighed, leaning on an old oak tree whose branches had been badly damaged by the storm.

For a while, Kyle was also at a loss over what to do.

But then he remembered his great-grandfather's treasure map. Though it had gotten a bit wet and smudged, Kyle could still read it. Perhaps it would show them a secret passage leading off the island. The two leaned down to study the yellow map. They stared at each other, then back at the map. It looked as if the treasure had been buried right here under the oak tree!

Kyle and Aurin started to dig furiously with shovels from the boat. At first they found only sand and stones, but just as the knight was ready to give up, his shovel hit something solid. It was a chest! The two treasure hunters carefully opened the small chest and found a trove of dusty bottles and a scribbled note that said:

Delicious! Wonderful!
Please try some
but just one sip at a time!
Knight Kasimir

Kyle groaned. "So there's no silver lance and no secret passageway, and I have enough old bottles like these in my basement already."

"Maybe there's some soda in them at least," Aurin said hopefully. He opened one bottle and carefully sipped the liquid inside. It tasted like raspberry and vanilla, with a bit of lemon, and Aurin thought he'd never had anything as delicious as this in all his elfin years.

Just as he was reaching for a second bottle, he felt a slight prickling on his skin. The next time Kyle looked at his friend he got a terrible shock, as now only half of Aurin was visible. He had vanished from the waist down. Aurin looked like half an elf hovering above the ground!

"Hmm, that's apparently a potion that makes you

invisible," said Kyle. "It's a little old, though, and doesn't work quite right." The knight recalled that his great-grandfather would often experiment with magic potions.

"Try this one," Kyle suggested, handing Aurin a bottle containing a green liquid.

It tasted like peppermint and chocolate. A few moments later, Aurin was completely visible again, but he was as tall as the oak tree standing next to him.

"Ah, let's try something else,"

Kyle said. Then he gave the elf the next bottle of colorful, sparkling liquid.

Taking turns after that, they tried a potion that made you smaller, one that made you sick to your stomach, another that turned you into a fish, and an especially delicious potion that gave you red stripes across your face. Finally they had just one bottle left.

"It's your turn again," Aurin said, handing Kyle the last bottle. Now, after drinking the sick-to-your-stomach potion, the elf had a tummy ache and was feeling somewhat woozy. He knew you shouldn't drink out of bottles when you don't know what's in them, but after all, these bottles were recommended by Kyle's great-grandfather.

Kyle took a sip and noticed he was rising from the ground like a soap bubble. After another careful sip, he heard a gurgling and hissing in his stomach, and he began to fly away like a gas-filled balloon.

"A real flying potion!" Kyle cried out to the elf, who was waving up at him. "Come on, follow me!"

Kyle threw the bottle down to Aurin. The elf took a

deep gulp, tucked the chest under his arm, and together they flew away, first over Willow Lake and then over all of Fairyland East. Beneath them the trees looked like matchsticks. They saw the village of Waldheim, Dragon Mountain, and even the faraway castle of the evil magician Balduin. Now and then they met a crow or a magpie that stared as these big, strange birds passed by.

Just before the potion wore off, they landed in the castle courtyard. Because the drink was very old, it gave them pink dots on their noses, but fortunately the spots disappeared after a few days. Kyle and Aurin gave the rest of the potions to Fairy Laureana but kept the flying potion for themselves, as they had enough left for a few more trips. Sometimes, when they were feeling sad, the

friends took deep gulps of it and flew away to where the sun sets behind Dragon Mountain, and one day they found an even greater treasure, and that was . . .

But wait, that's a story for another time.

The Birthday Tournament

When the first violets bloom in May, Knight Kyle celebrates his birthday. It's always a great party with an even greater tournament to which all the knights of the land are invited—from the snowy North, the torrid South, the rainy West, and the forested East, where Kyle's castle stands.

More than anything else, the knights look forward every year to seeing the lady of the castle, Constance, who lives high up in a tower room. Of course, they would never admit that, but now and then they peek up at the balcony where Constance likes to sit and read. If Lady Constance does see them, the knights puff out their chests and try to look especially gallant as they stride across the courtyard.

This year, once again, all the knights had exciting stories to tell of their voyages to distant places through snow, rain, and sweltering heat.

Knight Max, for example, had crossed stormy Dragon Mountain on horseback in just one night. Three dragons had been lying in wait for him there, but he'd driven them all off with his sword. Knight Bertram had crossed the sea in a magnificent sailing ship and had met five sea serpents that he frightened away just by loudly slamming the visor of his helmet. Finally, Knight Oswald told about the seventeen . . . oh, no, the *seventy* trolls, all

as tall as trees and armed with clubs, who had seen him in his gleaming, freshly polished suit of armor and were so dazzled that they fainted, crashed into each other, and fell to the ground.

The knights were sitting in the sun in front of the castle, boasting of their knightly deeds and looking forward to the tournament. Kyle had announced that the prize this year was a chocolate dragon egg made by the baker in Waldheim from only the finest ingredients. It gleamed even more than Oswald's armor and had a delectable fragrance. The egg was about as big as a football, filled with nougat, strawberries, and cream, wrapped in

crinkly golden paper, and displayed in a festive tent right in front of the castle. Now and then one of the knights entered the tent to admire the egg, his mouth watering.

None of these remarkably brave and clever knights realized that not far away, the robber Rasputin lay in wait, hiding behind a bush. He had watched as the egg was brought in on a wagon from Waldheim, through the forest and all the way to the castle.

Rasputin had a rusty sword, a fiery red hat with a broad brim that he was especially proud of, a shaggy beard, and a patch over one eye. He looked so ferocious that all he had to do was rattle his sword and roll his one eye, and people would run away from him. Because he'd always acted that way, he thought that was simply the way things had to bc. Sometimes he wished he could talk with some of the travelers, but since they always fled, he just took everything in their coaches and wagons to his cave, where he sat down among all his stolen treasure, alone. He wished he'd been invited to Kyle's birthday party, but he was much too proud to admit that out loud, and so he just continued to rob people.

Rasputin hadn't dared to rob the chocolate dragon egg while it was being brought to the castle, as Kyle had been riding alongside the carriage, and the robber was terrified of the knight. Kyle was the best sword fighter in the land, and he'd once grabbed Rasputin and cut off his beard so that Rasputin's face looked pale as a baby's bottom.

Now Rasputin was hiding behind a bush beside the castle, thinking feverishly about how he could steal the chocolate egg.

Hmm, I could just run out with my sword, let out a terrible roar, and roll my eye, he said to himself. *Maybe the knights will run away.*

But then he looked out at the knights with their gleaming armor, helmets, and long swords, and he shook his head sadly. The knights didn't look like they'd just run away.

Rasputin kept brooding over his problem until he

broke out in a sweat. Then all at once he grinned so broadly that the gold fillings in his teeth sparkled in the sunlight. He'd devised a devilish plan worthy of a robber.

A long time ago he'd attacked a coach that contained an old suit of armor with a helmet, a shield, and everything else. He'd taken the armor with him, without knowing what to do with it, and ever since then it had been gathering dust in his robber's den.

If I'm dressed as a knight, too, he thought, *these other guys in their tin suits won't recognize me, so I can grab the chocolate egg and run off!*

Rasputin chuckled into his scraggly beard, then snuck back to his lonely cave in the forest.

By now, the tournament was in full swing. In the jousting competition all the knights carried lances with rubber points so no one would get hurt as they rode toward each other on their horses and tried to throw off their opponents. Next, they fought with wooden swords and shot arrows at a dragon that Kyle had drawn with chalk on the castle wall.

Everyone had a lot of fun, and during the breaks they drank tons of cocoa and told each other the latest knight jokes—*Why was the army too tired to fight? They had a lot of sleepless knights!*—while peeking up at the balcony where Lady Constance was sitting in the sun, leafing through her book, and occasionally dozing off. She didn't care much for tournaments.

Early in the afternoon an unfamiliar knight arrived at the castle. He was riding a decrepit old donkey and his armor didn't look new, either. It was stained, battered,

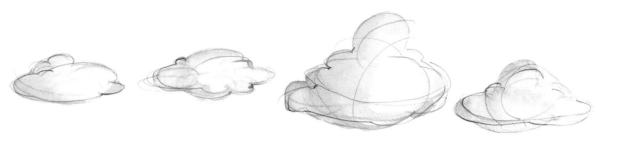

and rusted, and it creaked every time he moved, but the man in the armor was without doubt a knight.

Kyle set down his cup of cocoa and went to greet the stranger.

"Who are you?" he asked. "I've never seen you here before."

"Uh . . . I'm the forest knight."

"But why don't I know you?" Kyle asked.

"I'm, uh, new in the forest," the man said, trying to see through the rusty visor on his helmet. "I travel around a lot."

After the other knights had discussed the situation for a long time—it always took them a long time to discuss anything—Kyle returned to the stranger. "Well, if you wish, you can take part in our tournament," he said. "We could use another opponent."

Rasputin grinned inside his helmet, for that was exactly his plan.

"You silly tin men," he whispered to himself. "Hah! Now I'll get my hands on that chocolate egg!"

The robber tried to compete, but soon it was clear he had no chance against the real knights. He fell off his donkey a few times, fumbled with his sword, struggled to see through his visor, and finally sat down on the spectators' bench, saying he needed a rest.

Earlier, Rasputin had cut a long slit down the back of his armor, and now he slipped out, crawled under the bench, and snuck over to the tent with the chocolate dragon egg inside. His armor was still sitting on the bench, but no one could see that the robber was no longer in it.

The other knights noticed none of this and were still taking part in the tournament. With his rubber lance, Max had just thrown Bertram off his horse, and now Bertram was angry because he said he hadn't been ready. Oswald, who was Max's best friend, then called Bertram a bad sport, and in no time all the knights were fighting, just as real knights sometimes do. Lady Constance watched, just shaking her head.

"Knights!" she said with a sigh. "Why do they always have to fight?"

In the meantime, Rasputin cut a big hole in the back of the tent with his rusty sword, grabbed the chocolate dragon egg, and ran off.

The knights fought and fought until Bertram accidentally poked his lance into the armor of the unknown knight. With a clatter it fell over and broke into pieces, and now the knights could see the suit of armor was empty. They'd been tricked!

Fearing the worst, they ran to the tent, but it was too late. The dragon egg and the forest knight had disappeared!

"We were so busy fighting, we let someone steal our prize!" Kyle grumbled, turning bright red beneath his helmet, angry and embarrassed all at once. "Search the castle for him!"

41

The knights ran off in all directions, searching the four towers, the dungeon, the chimney, and even the outhouse, but the robber was nowhere to be found. Sadly, the knights returned to the courtyard and sank down on the seats of their freshly polished iron pants.

All of a sudden they heard a dreadful whining and groaning.

"*Ohhhoahhhhhoahhhoaaaah!*" someone was crying, and even the boldest knight now felt a bit afraid. "*Ohhhoahhhhhoahhhoaaaah!*" Again and again, louder and louder, came the sound.

"Once I battled a cryptic dragon up in the Troll Mountains. It sounded like that," Max whispered as he sank down a bit farther into his armor.

"Once, up on the Nebelhorn, I saw five witches flying by on their broomsticks, and that's the way they sounded," Bertram whispered as he closed his helmet and locked it with a padlock that had been specially made for him.

"Ohhhoahhhhhhoahhhoaaaah!" The knights heard it again, and they trembled.

That was too much for the lady of the castle. She put her book aside, came strutting down the stairs from the balcony, and walked straight to the well, where the whimpering and moaning were coming from.

"I think I know who our monster is," she said with a smile and waved to the fearful knights to come over. "Look for yourselves—the horrible monster is wearing a red hat and an eye patch."

And indeed, when the knights looked into the well, they didn't see a cryptic dragon or a witch on a broomstick, but the robber Rasputin cowering down below, soaking wet and wailing mournfully enough to soften their metal armor.

"My tummy hurts *sooooo* much!" he cried, his mouth smeared with chocolate from swallowing the dragon egg in one gulp.

The knights couldn't help but laugh, and none of

them wanted to admit to Constance that up until just a moment ago he was even a little bit afraid.

"It's your own fault!" Kyle called down the well. "Why did you have to go and steal our chocolate egg?"

"We should help him just the same," Constance declared. "Remember the terrible bellyache you had last year because you ate your whole birthday cake all by yourself? Besides, it's all *your* fault. Why do you always have to fight like that?"

"Because we're knights?" Kyle said. Like Rasputin, they'd always acted that way, so they thought that was simply the way things had to be.

Now Kyle took pity, too. Fortunately, he had some medicine from Fairy Laureana on hand, and he lowered the bottle down the well on a rope. The robber thanked him, drank it eagerly, and finally fell asleep, exhausted.

The knights celebrated Kyle's birthday all night long, even without the chocolate egg, and swore to the lady of the castle that they wouldn't fight all next week.

And they kept their promise for three full days.

The Invisible Magician

Far up on Dragon Mountain, where icy winds
howl and trees cannot grow, stands the castle
of Balduin the magician. Rocky cliffs tower
above a narrow, slippery path leading up
to the castle, and only very rarely does
anyone venture into this grim
place. Balduin is much
too mean to

have many friends, and only once in a while does he have his tame dragon, Gogol, or the robber Rasputin to keep him company. He spends most of his time in his laboratory or his library, where he sits for hours trying to figure out where Knight Kyle could have hidden the silver lance. Balduin believes he can rule over all of Fairyland if he can get his hands on it. He doesn't know that Kyle doesn't have the lance himself and thinks his great-grandfather Kasimir probably lost it on one of his adventures.

Balduin's most recent invention was a magic helmet with many hoses and knobs, and if you put it on and flipped a few switches, you could make yourself invisible.

"Just look at this, Gogol!" the magician cried. "I am the greatest!"

His pet dragon wearily opened one eye and yawned. He'd been chasing bats all night, and all he wanted to do now was sleep.

"With this devious device I'll finally get my hands on Kyle's silver lance," Balduin said, jumping for joy as he put on the helmet.

He flicked a few switches. There was a crackling sound, sparks flew, and in the wink of an eye the magician was invisible. Gogol didn't know any of this was happening, as he'd already gone back to sleep.

Meanwhile, everyone in Kyle's castle was celebrating Thursday. Kyle wasn't happy that you could have parties only on birthdays or on some other holiday, so he simply invented a new holiday—Thursday—and since Friday was practically the start of the weekend, and everyone celebrated weekends anyway, parties at Kyle's castle usually went on for several days.

As usual, Kyle had invited his best friends to the Thursday party, and everyone sat together in the throne room and played Excalibur, their favorite card game.

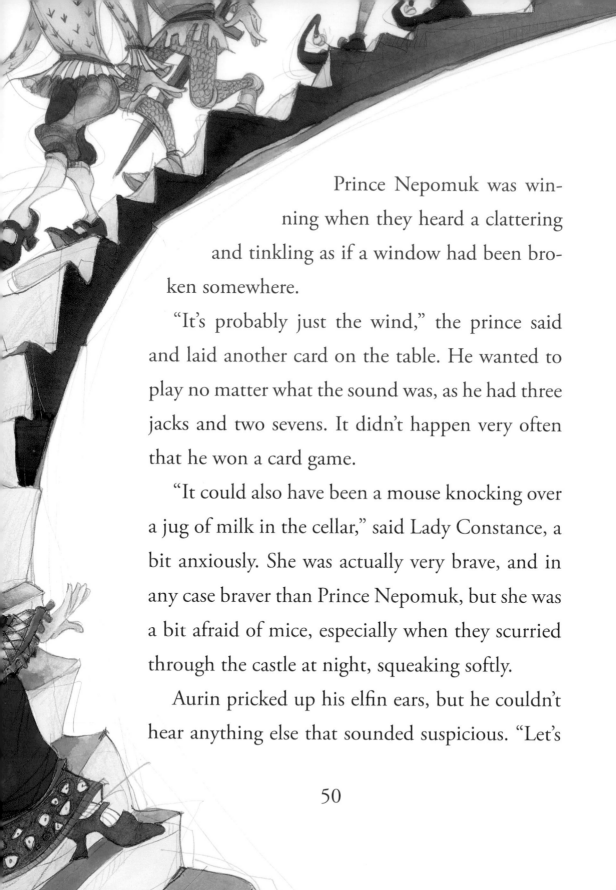

Prince Nepomuk was winning when they heard a clattering and tinkling as if a window had been broken somewhere.

"It's probably just the wind," the prince said and laid another card on the table. He wanted to play no matter what the sound was, as he had three jacks and two sevens. It didn't happen very often that he won a card game.

"It could also have been a mouse knocking over a jug of milk in the cellar," said Lady Constance, a bit anxiously. She was actually very brave, and in any case braver than Prince Nepomuk, but she was a bit afraid of mice, especially when they scurried through the castle at night, squeaking softly.

Aurin pricked up his elfin ears, but he couldn't hear anything else that sounded suspicious. "Let's

50

go and look tomorrow morning," he said, "when we don't have to fumble around in the dark. Anyway, I'd like to play one of my newest songs for you. It's a very sad ballad that—"

"Let's just go and check now," Kyle quickly interrupted. He really liked Aurin a lot, but his songs always made him so tired that he'd rather go down to a dark cellar and listen to the mice squeaking.

The group went down the stairs together and, after looking around, discovered a broken window in the storeroom. But that wasn't all. On the floor they found splintered glass and some spilled flour, and when Kyle examined the flour more closely, he could see white footprints leading into the next room.

They followed the prints over to the wine cellar, where someone had clearly been helping himself to the contents of a wine barrel. From there the prints started to fade as they led up to the main floor and into the armory. The

door to the armory was ajar, and the prince, the lady, the knight, and the elf could hear a frightful racket inside.

When they peeked through the crack, they saw something remarkable. The famous painting of Kasimir and the silver lance wasn't hanging straight on the wall, the weapons cabinet was open, and swords, axes, spears, and halberds were somehow flying out of it.

"I-Is it a ghost?" Nepomuk asked. The others, too, turned a little pale as a battle-ax whizzed by them.

"Definitely not! I think someone is trying to trick us," Kyle whispered. "Just wait."

The knight ran back to the storeroom without telling the others what he was doing.

The ghost was, of course, none other than Balduin the magician. While he was invisible, he'd broken into the castle through a cellar window, knocked over a flour sack, and drunk half a barrel of strawberry wine. Now he was slightly drunk and looking around the armory for the silver lance. Since he couldn't find it, he got angrier and angrier, pulling everything out of the cabinets and throwing the weapons on the ground. The magician was so angry he didn't notice the people outside the door.

"*Wheeere—hic!—iss thee ssssilverlannce?*" he mumbled. "*Eet* must be *heeere sssomewheere—hic!*"

Kyle had now come back from the storeroom with a barrel of flour and a big net.

"What are you going to do with that?" Prince Nepomuk whispered.

Kyle didn't answer but tore open the door to the armory and scattered the flour across the floor. The magician was invisible, but he left footprints in the flour everywhere he went, of course, and Kyle could clearly see now where he was.

"I've got you!" Kyle cried, throwing out the net, and indeed something invisible was thrashing about in it as

the net ran back and forth through the room like a wild
will-o'-the-wisp.

"Hah! I've caught you, and I'm coming to get you!"
Kyle stormed into the room.

A couple of times he missed, clutching at nothing
but thin air, but then he shouted triumphantly and the
helmet became visible in his hand. At that moment the
magician also became visible and struggled like a fish in
the knight's net.

"Let me go! Let me go at once!" Balduin screeched.

"This isn't fair." But Kyle and his friends just wrapped him up tighter in the net.

"We've caught a fine fish!" Aurin laughed.

"A very fat one," added Nepomuk. "And a tipsy one at that. He swam right through the strawberry wine and straight to us. Let's throw him back in the water, where he belongs."

They all dragged the magician and the net to the nearby river, counted to three, and threw him in a wide arc out into the water. Then they returned to the castle for their Thursday party and their game of cards.

The magician clung on to a large branch floating down the river until he managed to reach the shore; then

he hobbled the whole long way back to his castle. He arrived dripping wet and had Gogol light a fire for him in the fireplace and then make him buckets and buckets of hot chamomile tea. Just the same, Balduin had a cold for two months and never again drank strawberry wine.

From then on Kyle used the magic helmet only as a flowerpot, and in it grew the most beautiful invisible narcissus in all of Fairyland.

The Lost Book of Magic

Right next to Kyle's castle in the forest lives the Fairy Laureana. No one can remember how long she's lived there. For ages she's been sitting in her lopsided cabin, brewing magic potions and helping the animals. If a fox breaks a leg or a mouse nibbles on a poison mushroom, if a squirrel falls from a tree or a woodpecker complains about a headache from all his picking and pecking, they come to her to be cured. If Knight Kyle or one of his friends is sick, Fairy Laureana packs her medicine bag, flies straight up to the castle, and prescribes something that tastes horrible but works miracles.

One day Kyle had a tummy ache because he'd eaten too much strawberry pie the night before, so Laureana headed up to the castle.

Because she was a bit old and forgetful, however, she left her front door open. The robber Rasputin happened to be nearby and noticed the open door. For a long time he'd wanted to break into the fairy's house, so as soon as she left, Rasputin snuck in. It was dark inside, with lots of bottles, pots, and pans of all shapes and sizes on the shelves. In the middle of the room a rusty kettle hung over the hearth, and on a table along the back wall lay a big open book.

The robber groped his way through the house, found the book, and started leafing through it. Then he giggled and rubbed his dirty hands with glee.

"The fairy's book of magic!" he exclaimed. "And Laureana just leaves it lying around here? Well, then she has only herself to blame."

Rasputin, you see, once

wanted to be a magician himself, and when he saw the book of magic before him, he imagined he could become the mightiest magician of all time. Rasputin the Great! Even greater than Balduin. Who knows, he might even find a spell to locate Kyle's silver lance and sell it to Balduin for lots of money. He stuffed his loot in his dirty robber's sack and ran away as fast as his robber's feet would carry him.

But he didn't notice a little bed in a corner of the house with a raccoon in it, hiding under the straw and hay. The furry patient had sprained his paw while digging for worms and would now have to wear a big bandage and stay in bed for three days. He had been watching everything from his corner.

"Oh no, oh no!" the raccoon whimpered. "If the robber steals the book, the fairy can no longer conjure up cures with her magic. He's certainly up to no good, and I've got to warn Laureana."

On his three good paws the raccoon hobbled the whole way through the forest to the castle. Panting heavily, he knocked, and soon Kyle opened the door. The fairy's medicine had truly worked wonders on the knight. He was secretly nibbling on another piece of strawberry pie, even though Laureana had strictly forbidden it.

The knocking also woke up the fairy, who was taking a nap in Kyle's guest room. At first she didn't know who made her angrier: Kyle for eating the strawberry pie or the raccoon for running through the forest despite her orders to stay in bed.

"If you keep on like this," she said, scolding the dog, "your paw will never heal."

But the wheezing raccoon interrupted her. "Your magic book . . . The robber Rasputin . . . He stole it!"

When Fairy Laureana heard this, she almost fainted. The book contained all the formulas she had written down in her entire life.

Kyle ran to his horse, saddled it, picked up the fairy, and away they rode at a full gallop, even faster than the fairy could fly.

On the road to Waldheim, they turned into the forest just after crossing the bridge, because Kyle knew where to find the robber's cave. The cave appeared damp and dark, and no fire was visible inside. As quietly as possible, Kyle drew his sword and crept in.

Fairy Laureana followed, her knees trembling. She'd never been in a robber's den, and this looked like a pretty bad one. The walls were all sooty, and the floor was a mess, with Rasputin's loot strewn everywhere. Boxes were broken apart, sacks were slit open, and the smell of mildew and gunpowder hung in the air. Somewhere far off in the forest they could hear a crow calling; otherwise there was nothing but silence.

"It seems he's not home," Kyle whispered.

The fairy was glad to hear that, because even though she could perform magic, she was still afraid of the robber and the wild stories about him.

"Then let's hurry up and go," she whispered back. "Maybe he's lying in wait for us outside the cave and . . ." But then something occurred to her. "I hope he didn't take the book to Balduin!" she said, sobbing, and began to quiver all over at the very thought that the evil magician might have her book now and run around the country performing acts of black magic.

At that moment they both heard a strange sound.

"*Ribbit!*" Then again: "*Ribbit!*"

Kyle looked around the cave, and in a dark corner behind one of the crates he discovered the magic book! It was lying open on the ground, and on top sat a small, slimy green frog with very sad eyes that reminded him of something or someone he knew.

"*Ribbit!*" the frog croaked again. He hopped up to the knight and appeared to be desperately trying to tell him something. "*Ribbit, ribbit!*"

All of a sudden, Fairy Laureana started laughing. "That must be the robber Rasputin!" she cried out with relief. "He turned himself into a frog, and now he doesn't know how to change himself back."

The frog seemed to be struggling to read a few words from the magic book, but the only sound coming out of his mouth was "*Ribbit, ribbit, ribbit!*"

Kyle picked up the frog carefully and gazed into his sad eyes. "Hello, robber," he said. "Shall we change you back, or would

you rather remain a slimy little green frog? What do you think?"

"*Ribbit, ribbit!*" the frog responded frantically.

"Will you promise never to steal a magic book again?" Kyle asked. "Cross your heart?"

"*Ribbbbitttt!*" croaked the frog and nodded his green head vigorously.

"I think we can change him back," Kyle said, winking at the fairy. "He gave me his word of honor as a frog."

Laureana touched the frog with her wand and spoke the words that were at the very end of the big book of magic.

"Spider leg and witch's broom! Your former self you will resume!"

There was a loud bang, then dazzling flashes of light and thick clouds of smoke, and for a moment all they could see in the robber's cave were stars in front of their eyes. When the smoke cleared, none other than the robber Rasputin stood before them, but with one difference:

from head to foot he was green as a frog. It appeared the fairy's spell hadn't worked quite right.

"*Ribbit!*" the robber was about to say, but then it occurred to him that now he could talk again. "*Ribbit*, uh, thank you," he said. "I'll never steal a book of magic again. I give you my word of honor . . . as a robber."

Then he looked down and noticed in horror that his body was as green as grass. He ran out into the forest and jumped into a pond, but no matter how much he washed and scrubbed, he remained green—for two whole weeks. He was so embarrassed, he didn't venture out of his den the whole time, and every traveler felt safe during that time.

Meanwhile, the frogs in the pond had taken a great liking to the green robber, and for many nights afterward they sat in front of his cave, croaking and keeping the robber awake.

The Black Dragon Tooth

One dark night, Kyle woke with a start and sat straight up in bed. An earsplitting noise was echoing through the castle: "Ooh! Ahhh!" It was an awful sound, so loud that sleep was out of the question.

Kyle donned his armored bathrobe and rushed down the stairs into the courtyard, where a sleepy-looking Prince Nepomuk and Lady Constance were staring out

into the darkness, try-
ing to discover who or
what was making such a
racket.

"Hello, Kyle," the prince said after
a big yawn. Despite the late hour he was
still wearing a silver crown on his freshly
brushed wig. "Do you have any idea who is
making this terrible noise? Whoever it is, he should
be thrown into the deepest dungeon for this behavior!"

Kyle just shrugged drowsily, but then suddenly they
all heard a flapping of wings approaching, and Arthur
the eagle landed on the ramparts of the castle's south
tower.

"*Caw!*" he croaked, then stopped to preen his feathers. "I came here—*caw*—from Dragon Mountain.
Dragobert needs your help. Please do something to stop
this racket. None of the animals can sleep!"

Dragobert was a kind dragon who lived in a cave;
he was one of Kyle's oldest friends. Kyle had once saved

him from the clutches of the magician Balduin, who had locked the dragon in a cage when he was very young and tried to train him to light the fire in his stove. Now Dragobert was as big as a barn and helped Kyle out whenever he could.

"What happened?" Kyle asked Arthur, who by now had finished preening his wings and was nibbling on a few cookies that Constance held out to him. Between bites he told them that Dragobert had a terrible toothache, and that was the reason for all the shouting. The dragon urgently needed someone to pull out his festering tooth.

"Let's go right away to help him," said Constance. "We can forget about sleeping now, anyway."

The three friends got dressed, mounted their horses, and set out to visit the diamond dwarfs, who lived at the foot of Dragon Mountain. Kyle's great-grandfather Kasimir had once come to the aid of the dwarfs in the great war against the trolls, and in return they gave him the famous magic silver lance, which had been missing now for as long as anyone could remember.

When they told the diamond dwarfs about Dragobert's sore tooth, the dwarfs at once fired up their blacksmith's forge and with much pounding and hammering made a pair of pliers as long and thick as an oak tree. (Living so close to the dragon, the dwarfs were also extremely eager to put an end to the noise.) Then Kyle and his friends loaded the pliers on a wagon and headed for the dragon's cave.

The howling and yammering was now so loud that no one could hear themselves speak.

"*Draaagggooobert!*" Kyle called out, trying to be heard over the noise, while Constance put her hands over her ears. "*Draaagggooobert!*"

Finally the dragon came crawling out of his cave, looking like a shamed puppy. His cheek was as swollen as a hot-air balloon, and tears dripped down his face, sizzling as they fell to the ground. He looked very, very miserable.

"It hurts *soooooo* much," he whimpered. He opened his huge mouth, and his friends could see a pitch-black stump way in the back.

"Don't worry. We'll help you," Prince Nepomuk said. "Soon it will all be over."

They chopped down a few trees near the cave with the help of the elves, and with ropes, screws, and nails Kyle and Nepomuk built a wooden tower in order to reach the dragon's tooth. But when they put the pliers into his mouth to pull it out, Dragobert couldn't control himself and spat out a jet of fire, just as dragons always do when they fight or feel they're in danger. The tower caught fire and fell over, and only at the last second were Kyle, Constance, and the prince able to jump down from the burning beams.

Kyle brushed the ashes from his armor. "This isn't going to work. We've got to come up with something else. But what?"

He called to Arthur the eagle and told him to hurry and get Elf Aurin and Fairy Laureana.

A few hours passed, and the dragon kept howling and whining so loudly that the mountains quavered. When the other friends arrived, they all talked about what to do, which was rather difficult, since Dragobert was roaring so much they had to shout at each other or use sign language.

Finally they came up with a plan. As usual, Aurin had brought the harp he used to sing the animals to sleep at Willow Lake. Now he started playing a lullaby so sweet the friends would have nodded off at once if they hadn't made sure to stuff parsley in their ears. Dragobert closed one eye, then the other, and he yawned while little blue flames flickered on his lips. Then his huge head fell forward, and he was asleep.

"Now we can begin," Kyle whispered.

They pried open Dragobert's jaws with two tree trunks, and carefully Kyle

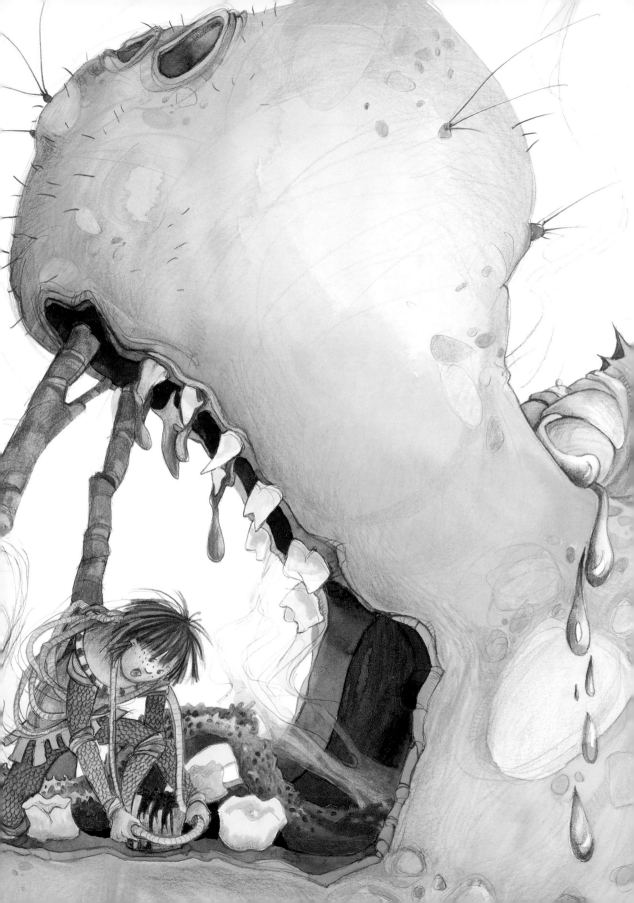

crawled inside. It stank of sulfur, ashes, and rancid milk, and Kyle prayed the tree trunks would hold up and he wouldn't be eaten alive if the sleeping dragon's jaws accidentally snapped shut.

Kyle slipped a few times on Dragobert's scaly tongue, clung tightly to his deadly fangs, and ducked when boiling dragon spit dripped down beside him. Way in the back he saw a dreadfully dark hole.

Anyone falling down there would wind up in the dragon's stomach for sure.

Kyle finally reached the black tooth, tied a thick rope around it, and ran out of the dragon's mouth. Then his friends tied the rope around Kyle's horse. Rosinante pulled and pulled, and at first nothing happened, but just as the friends were about to give up, the tooth came loose and crashed onto the rocky floor in front of the cave.

"You did it!" shouted Constance, Aurin, and Nepomuk. "Three cheers for our brave Sir Kyle!" Kyle turned a bit red with embarrassment.

But the work still wasn't over. Kyle had to reenter Dragobert's mouth, this time with a barrel full of medicine from Fairy Laureana that he poured over the wound. Steaming and hissing, the hole closed up.

As fast as his legs would carry him, Kyle joined the others outside to wait for the dragon to wake up. A long time passed before Dragobert stretched and looked at his friends with sleepy eyes. Just as he was about to let out another mighty roar of pain, a broad smile appeared on his face.

"My toothache!" he cried. "My toothache is gone." He spread his wings and joyously flew five times around the volcano by his cave. When he landed, a wagon was rumbling up the narrow road.

"These are the diamond dwarfs," Kyle said. "They brought you something, Dragobert."

The dwarfs wheeled a big, long crate up to the cave entrance and told Dragobert he could open the present himself. Inside the crate was a toothbrush—a real dragon's toothbrush—as long as a drawbridge, with bristles of sparkling silver wire.

"You see, nobody wants to be wakened by your shouts in the middle of the night," said Aurin with a smile.

Dragobert promised to brush his teeth every morning and every night from now on, and not to eat so much candy. He gave his black dragon tooth to Lady Constance, who had it covered in gold and used it as a stool at her dressing table until it finally found its way to the castle museum.

Trollaby and Good Night

When summer comes to Fairyland East, the animals and plants don their finest clothes. The flowers put forth red, blue, and yellow blossoms; trees wave their green branches in the wind; and the birds, mice, rabbits, and deer—and even the dirty, smelly wild pigs—get all spruced up. To welcome the start of summer, Lady Constance wears her dress that gleams like golden-yellow pollen and sets a wreath of nasturtiums in her hair.

This year Constance wanted to greet the summer from up on Dawn Rock, which is where the first sunlight of the morning appears in Fairyland East. It lies very close

to the Troll's Teeth, a few barren, rocky hills on the road to Waldheim. Not many travelers ever venture there.

When Constance told Kyle of her plan, he shook his head uneasily.

"That's where the trolls live, and as you know, they are not to be trifled with," he said. "Even if they are terribly dumb, you have to really watch out for them."

That was certainly the case. Trolls *are* dumb, but each one is as strong as ten men. Their skin is made of granite. When these monsters are asleep, you don't know if a troll is lying on the ground or if you're standing at the foot of a hill.

"I can watch out for myself," Constance replied snappily. "Anyway, the trolls surely won't be awake that early."

The next morning she set out long before dawn, and after a while she arrived at the Troll's Teeth. It was still pitch-black, but after some searching Constance found Dawn Rock standing out like a dark shadow above all the other rocks. As she was a good climber, Constance

soon reached the top, but she wasn't a second too early; the warm sun was just rising above the forest.

"Hello, summer!" she cried excitedly. "Here I am. Greetings, and please bring us this year—" She suddenly stopped, hearing a grating sound nearby, as if a large rock were scraping along an even larger rock.

Then she heard a deep voice: "Summer? I don't be called Summer—I be called Quartzclump."

Constance knew as soon as she heard the voice that it had to be a troll on an early-morning walk.

She tried to climb down from the rock quickly and quietly, but just then a huge face appeared on top of the rock. She hadn't climbed Dawn Rock

at all. She'd climbed a troll! It was as tall as a castle tower, had stone-cold eyes, and was looking down on her as if she were a bug. An icy-gray hand reached for her and lifted her up for a closer look.

"Hah! You be present for my daughter," said the troll. "You be sweet little puppet."

"Hey! I'm no sweet little puppet," Constance yelled. "I'm the lady of a castle, and when Knight Kyle hears about this, you'll be in big trouble."

She tried to wriggle free from the troll's clutches, but it was like she was completely enclosed in rock.

Growling, Quartzclump

carried her to his cave, where he lived with his troll wife and his little troll daughter. His wife was busy making lava soup on a small volcano in the middle of the cave.

"Lava soup, ugh!" said the little troll girl, who was actually as large as a swamp birch. "Me want chocolate and stone dust!"

Her mother paid no attention to her complaints and kept stirring the pot, from which clouds of black-and-gray smoke were rising.

"Me want chocolate and stone dust!" the troll child repeated, stamping her foot with every word so that the whole cave shook and the pot threatened to fall over.

"*Whaaaa!*" she bawled. "*Arrrggghhh!*"

It sounded like a summer thunderstorm, so loud that Constance had to hold her ears.

Quartzclump walked over, crunched his rocky face into a grimace, and handed the struggling lady to his daughter.

"Here, a gift," he said proudly. "Now you no more whine."

The girl stopped crying at once and pressed Constance firmly to her stony chest.

"Hey, watch out, you clumsy piece of rock," Constance shouted. "You'll crush me to death."

The troll child now carefully took Constance in her arms like a baby, humming and babbling as she rocked her new doll, softly singing her a trollaby. Finally, she placed Constance on a bed of moss and covered her gently with some damp, rotting leaves.

When the lady of the castle tried to sit up, the girl growled threateningly and raised her finger, then she tied Constance to a rocky outcrop with a thick rope.

"You be good," the girl said, "or no dessert."

"What have I gotten myself into?" Constance moaned to herself as she tried to hold back tears. "Kyle warned me! Now I can only hope he finds me here and helps me escape."

But Knight Kyle had gone swimming that day in Willow Lake with Prince Nepomuk and Elf Aurin. He'd removed his armor and was splashing around with his friends; still, he kept looking up at the sun moving west-ward across a cloudless sky. As it slowly began to get dark, Kyle became anxious.

"Constance should have returned long ago from her summer walk. I hope nothing has happened to her," he said to the others.

"Maybe she's already back at the castle," Nepomuk replied.

"But then she would have passed this way," said Kyle. "I think we should go look for her in the Troll's Teeth, even if it's dangerous."

They quickly got dressed and started on their way. When they reached the mountains, it was the middle of the night, and there was no trace of Constance.

"Constance!" Aurin cried. "Are you here

somewhere?" But no one replied, and all they could hear were a few small stones falling into a deep ravine somewhere.

"I hope she didn't fall from Dawn Rock," said Nepomuk. "But I can't imagine it. She's such a good climber."

They searched and searched until they heard a growling and scraping nearby.

"Those are the trolls," Kyle whispered. "Let's check to make sure everything is all right."

They crept past some large rocks and saw the entrance to a cave in front of them. Inside they could see the flickering light of a fire and hear a rumbling and pounding.

"How often do I have to tell you I'm not a doll!" said a familiar voice inside the cave. "Can't you finally get that into your thick quartz skull? And I also don't want to eat any lava soup."

"That's definitely Constance," whispered Aurin. "The trolls have captured her."

The friends hid behind a fallen tree and watched the troll family sitting around the fire.

The troll girl held Constance tightly in her fist and tried to feed her a giant spoonful of steaming, bubbling soup. Since Constance steadfastly refused to open her mouth, the child put her new doll back on the bed of moss and tied the rope around her leg again to make sure she didn't run away. The troll girl grumbled, scolding Constance and shaking her head in disappointment.

"Bad puppet," she said. "You go sleep now. Today no dessert."

"We've got to free Constance right away," Kyle whispered, "before this troll tries to feed her lava soup again."

"And just how will you do that?" Nepomuk asked. "We're much too small to fight trolls."

Kyle stared into the cave, where the flames were still dancing and flickering, then nodded slowly. "If we're too small, then we just have to make ourselves bigger. Quick! Let's light a big fire out here behind these large boulders, where the trolls can't see us."

"Everyone knows that trolls aren't afraid of fire," Aurin objected, but Kyle had already begun to gather dry wood and put it in a pile.

When the pile was large enough, Kyle took out his matches and set fire to the wood. Soon it was burning so brightly that the mountainsides all around glowed as if being warmed by the morning sun.

"Now, both of you dance, right behind the fire," Kyle said, "while I go to the cave to free Constance."

"You want us to dance?" Nepomuk stared at him with his mouth wide open. "Are you completely out of your mind?"

But Aurin nodded enthusiastically, because he already understood Kyle's plan. As the elf and the prince started dancing behind the fire, huge shadows appeared on the mountainsides behind them. Aurin and Nepomuk looked like giants on the mountains!

When Quartzclump noticed the moving shadows in front of the cave, his stony brow furrowed.

"Who there?" he growled. "Other trolls? What they want?"

"Hah! You dumb rocks," Aurin said in a deep voice. "We're coming to crush you." And he lifted up a branch, casting a shadow as large as a tree on the cliff behind him.

"*Whaaat?*" Quartzclump bellowed. "Me only dumb rock? Bah! I crush you into tiny stones."

He stormed out of the cave, his wife and daughter following angrily. Trolls like to fight; since they're made of stone, it doesn't hurt very much when they get hit.

As the three trolls came charging

toward their oppo-
nents, Kyle snuck
into the cave and
soon found Constance.

"Kyle!" she cried. "I
was beginning to think I'd

always be a troll's puppet." She was still tied to the bed of moss.

"Shh," he whispered, and started hacking at the thick rope with his sword.

The trolls ran around outside, trying to catch the shadows on the cliff, but whenever they reached out, the shadows darted to the side or disappeared and then reappeared in a completely different spot.

"You're as dirty as bat boogers!" Nepomuk shouted in a booming voice. "And as slow as turtles."

That was too much for Quartzclump, who barreled headfirst at the shadowy figure, smashing into the rock cliff so hard he started a few avalanches, burying himself and his family. But it wasn't over yet; the trolls just started digging themselves out.

"Kyle had better finish soon, or we'll be finished ourselves," Nepomuk grumbled. "We can't keep up this act much longer."

At that moment, the knight finally cut through the rope and ran out of the cave with Constance. He called to Nepomuk and Aurin to follow them; then they scrambled over piles of rock and ran through deep, narrow valleys, until they reached Willow Lake, and only then did they feel safe.

"I'm so sorry, Kyle," Constance gasped. "I should have listened to you."

Kyle grinned. "Really? I think life as a doll wouldn't have been so bad. You had a bed of moss, a loving troll mother, and a spoonful of hot lava soup every night. Maybe we should take you back?"

Constance was furious, and she was about to throw him in the lake when the sun began to rise over the forest. The four friends stood still and watched. The sunrise wasn't quite as beautiful as up on Dawn Rock—but it was a lot safer.

They swam all morning and half the afternoon in Willow Lake. Now and then they heard a far-off pounding and grinding because the not-so-clever trolls were still looking for the shadows and kept running into the cliffs.

Party Crashers

One fine Sunday morning in August, as Knight Kyle was sitting on the castle terrace enjoying a cup of cocoa with the lady of the castle and Prince Nepomuk, Arthur the eagle landed on their breakfast table. In his beak was a letter from Knight Max, who lived on the other side of Dragon Mountain.

"An invitation for you," Arthur cawed, eyeing the milk he'd just spilled when he landed.

Arthur had flown the whole long way over the mountains without stopping, and now he was understandably hungry. Constance handed him a chocolate croissant that he dipped into the puddle of milk with his left claw, while Kyle opened the envelope.

"We've been invited to Max's birthday party," he announced happily. "But it's tomorrow. How can we get to the other side of Dragon Mountain that quickly?"

Nepomuk frowned. "We can ask Dragobert, can't we? Maybe he'll fly us there."

Dragobert owed Kyle a favor ever since he pulled the dragon's sore tooth, and Arthur fluttered off to Dragobert's lair to tell him what the friends wanted. The dragon agreed at once to help. A half hour later the dragon landed noisily on the castle wall. The three passengers packed a picnic basket, and then off they went.

"Hold on tight!" Dragobert called, spreading his wings. The castle, the forest, and the road to Waldheim grew smaller and smaller, and soon the friends could see all of Fairyland East below them. Dragon Mountain grew closer and closer with each beat of Dragobert's mighty

wings. They saw the first snowcapped peaks below them, and it became cold even though it was still late summer down in the valley. Constance pulled her coat tighter around her and sang along with Dragobert's happy song about flowers and sunshine. Kyle and the prince spent the time telling jokes and playing guessing games.

Nepomuk was just about to ask Kyle the name of the great volcano right below them when he noticed a dot that appeared on the horizon behind them. The dot rapidly drew closer.

"Is it another dragon?" asked Constance.

"Maybe it's Arthur coming to tell us we've forgotten something," said the prince.

Soon they realized that it was neither an eagle nor a dragon, but a flying carpet, and on it sat a familiar figure—none other than Balduin the magician, who had secretly been following them! He approached at full speed from behind, and Dragobert was just able to get out of the way. Constance nearly fell off the dragon's back, and only at the last moment was Kyle able to catch her by her scarf.

"Hah! If you crash up here, I'll have all the time in the world to fetch the silver lance from the castle." Balduin laughed as he prepared to swoop down again, causing Dragobert to go into a dangerous tailspin. "It will take you weeks to get back home."

"Be careful!" Kyle shouted, but it was too late. The dragon had failed to notice a mountain peak, which he hit with his right wing, then spun around a few times, tumbled head over tail, and finally plummeted with his friends toward a snowy slope. There was a clattering and banging, then Kyle passed out.

When he came to, he felt as cold as if he were in the freezer at his castle. He opened his eyes and thought at

first he was blind, because everything around him was white. But then he realized that they had crashed in a deep, snow-filled valley. To his left lay a huge snowdrift with only the prince's crown on top, and alongside it, one end of Constance's scarf was sticking out of the snow.

Quickly the knight began digging with his sword, and soon he'd dug out the lady and the prince. They were coughing and spitting out snow, but they were not injured. Where was Dragobert?

They heard a whimpering farther down in the valley and stomped through the snow to get there, falling a few times and rolling downhill like snowballs. When they arrived at the bottom, covered with snow and soaking wet, they found the dragon. He had gotten wedged between some rocks and had broken his right wing, which hung limply at his side like a wet rag. As hard as he tried, Dragobert couldn't move.

"Oh, we're stuck here!" Nepomuk cried. "Without Dragobert we'll never get out."

Constance was trembling all over, as she was wearing only the thin dress made of pressed lily blossoms she'd chosen for Max's birthday party and her scarf. The coat she'd worn earlier had been lost in the crash.

The friends sat alongside Dragobert, their teeth chattering from the cold. Then Kyle had an idea. "Let's go and fetch some wood to build a sled!"

"Good plan," Constance replied as she jumped up and started looking around for trees and branches.

But no matter how hard they looked, they couldn't find any wood—there was nothing but snow, everywhere.

Dragobert stretched his ice-covered head and groaned. "Let me breathe some fire. I think I'm still able to do that."

He spat out a few blue flames, melting some snow. Beneath the snow they found twigs and branches, even

100

entire trees that had been blown down in an earlier storm.

After a brief search, the friends had found enough large tree trunks, which they carefully lashed together with Constance's long woolen scarf. It looked like an enormous raft in a sea of snow.

Dragobert was much too weak to crawl onto the sled, so everyone pulled and pushed the dragon until his huge body was resting on the tree trunks. Nepomuk and Constance crawled onto Dragobert's back while Kyle pushed the sled. As it started to move, the knight jumped onto the dragon's head and clung to his scaly neck. "Hold on!" cried Kyle. "Here we go."

The sled went faster and faster until they were racing down the slope like a rocket. They sailed off cliffs as if they were ski jumps and whizzed past stands of mountain pine. Constance's hair flew in the wind, and though she was a bit afraid, she thought the trip was a blast.

"Yoo-hoo! Clear the way! Here
we come!" Prince Nepomuk leaned
into the curves like a professional bobsledder.

Finally, they were approaching Fairyland Forest, and
what did they see? Between the trees a man was jumping
up and down—it was Balduin the magician! His flying
carpet had crashed shortly after the wild chase, and he
was now struggling to pick it up.

"Hey, watch out! We have no brakes!" shouted Kyle.

But it was too late. The sled, the dragon, the knight,
the prince, and the lady collided with Balduin, throwing

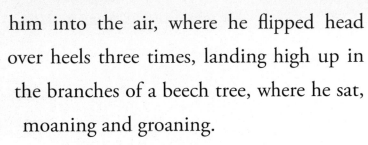

him into the air, where he flipped head over heels three times, landing high up in the branches of a beech tree, where he sat, moaning and groaning.

"Help me! I can't get down from here!" cried Balduin.

But even if the friends had wanted

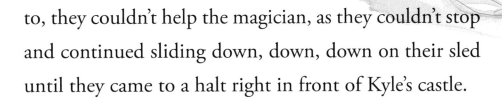

to, they couldn't help the magician, as they couldn't stop and continued sliding down, down, down on their sled until they came to a halt right in front of Kyle's castle.

"Man, oh man, wasn't that some ride!" Nepomuk said, wiping the sweat from his forehead as he climbed down from the dragon's back. "Even faster than my skateboard."

"And even more fun." Constance giggled. "We should do this more often."

Kyle went to see Fairy Laureana to tell her about the injured dragon. She helped Dragobert as best she could, with a gob of ointment, crushed linden blossoms, and twenty yards of dressing for his wounds. The dragon had to go back and stay in his lair for two weeks and wasn't allowed to fly, but every day his friends brought five apple cakes and a bucket of hot cocoa to his bedside.

And so it was that Kyle had to give Arthur the eagle a letter for Knight Max explaining why they couldn't come to his party.

Meanwhile, the magician Balduin crouched high up in the beech tree for hours trying to teach his carpet how to fly again.

"Hocus-pocus *dominocus*," he kept cackling. "Fly, fly, fly!"

But the carpet had a few big holes that couldn't be repaired, so Balduin shinnied down the tree—very slowly and very carefully—and hobbled back to his castle with the magic carpet tucked under his arm.

Ever since then, the carpet has remained by Balduin's fireplace. Now and then it starts to rise a few inches, crackling and puffing and sending up little clouds of dust, but it no longer has any desire to fly. Perhaps it's too cold outside and the carpet prefers just to be a comfy blanket to cuddle up in by the fire.

Kyle's Sensational Circus

Every autumn, the circus comes to Waldheim. It's always a big show, and everyone in Fairyland is invited. For weeks, Kyle and his friends had been very excited, and they were all wondering which tricks the circus artists would perform this year. There were tightrope walkers, ponies that danced in a circle, a strong man who could tear apart chains, two clowns, talking birds, camels that could do arithmetic in their heads, a toothless lion, a juggler with brightly colored balls, and much more.

As they did every year, Kyle, Aurin, Nepomuk, and Constance set out for the circus very early in the morn-

ing, but when they arrived at noon, they saw at once that something was different this time. The villagers gathered around the circus tent with sorrowful faces, a few children were crying and tugging at their mothers' skirts, and people were shaking their heads in disappointment.

Well, what's the matter here? Kyle wondered. *They all look like they've just had four weeks of bad weather.*

Constance tapped a man on the shoulder and asked what was wrong.

"Oh, it's so sad," he replied. "There will be no circus this year, as all the artists have coughs and colds and must stay in bed for the next few days. Even the lion has the chills."

Despite the cool autumn temperature, all the performers had gone swimming in the lake the day before, which only made their colds worse. Now Kyle and his friends spotted the sign at the entrance to the big tent that read, in large letters:

WE REGRET THE CIRCUS IS
CANCELED DUE TO ILLNESS

"I can't believe it," Kyle said. "All year we've been looking forward to the circus, and now look what happened!"

They all went to see the ringmaster and found him sitting sadly in his wagon, sniffling and sneezing.

"I am sorry," he said, as he kept wiping his nose, "but Fairy Laureana ordered all of us to stay in bed, and

we can't walk on tightropes or juggle in bed—*achoo!*"
He sneezed loudly a few more times, then continued.
"The fairy thought that laughter was the best medicine.
But how can we laugh when everyone outside is so sad?
Achoo!" He took out his big red handkerchief and blew
his nose while Kyle thought long and hard. Finally, the
knight clapped his hands for attention.

"I have a solution," he said. "If the circus performers
can't do their tricks, we'll do them ourselves!"

"You?" The ringmaster stared at them. "Can you
dance on tightropes and juggle balls?"

"Hmm, maybe we can't dance on ropes," said
Nepomuk, who at once took a liking to Kyle's idea,
"but I'm pretty good at skateboarding and can even do a
handstand on it."

"I could ride Rosinante standing up," Constance
said. She had never actually done that, but she'd always
wanted to try.

"And I can perform with a bow and arrow," Aurin
added. "And with my harp I could also—"

"Oh, I don't think we need any music today," Kyle quickly interrupted, "but I'm sure you'll be a real hit with your bow. I can perform my famous sword dance, and then"—he winked at the others—"for my grand finale I have a big surprise."

The ringmaster thought it over for a minute, then he nodded. "Very well, I'll announce your performances. But then I'll have to—*achoo!*—go right back to bed."

The friends gathered everything they needed for their tricks as the audience waited expectantly in the tent. Constance was especially excited when she saw all the people.

"If I'd known this was going to happen, I'd have put on a nicer dress," she whispered, peering out through a gap in the curtains. She was wearing a red-and-gold dress that was actually very nice. "My hair is a mess, too."

Kyle grinned. "You look spectacular, like a real circus artist, and your hair is combed almost as perfectly as Rosinante's mane."

"Well, thanks, I think," said Constance.

A few moments later, the ringmaster stepped into the tent, sniffled a few more times, then announced the new circus troupe with great fanfare.

"Today you will experience a *senssssation* unlike any the world has ever seen!" he declared. "Please welcome the circus of Kyle the knight!" He bowed deeply.

The crowd applauded as Elf Aurin entered the ring with his bow.

The elf could hit any target, no matter how small, and as a finale shot a candied apple from the head of the

Waldheim candy maker, which was followed by much applause. Next, Kyle performed his famous sword dance, in which he flung five wooden swords through the air at the same time as a chocolate cake, dividing it into little slices that he handed out, bowing repeatedly to his appreciative audience.

Then came Prince Nepomuk, who circled the
tent on his skateboard, faster and faster, until
the audience became dizzy. After that
he managed to wave at them while
doing a handstand, and the audience broke out in applause.

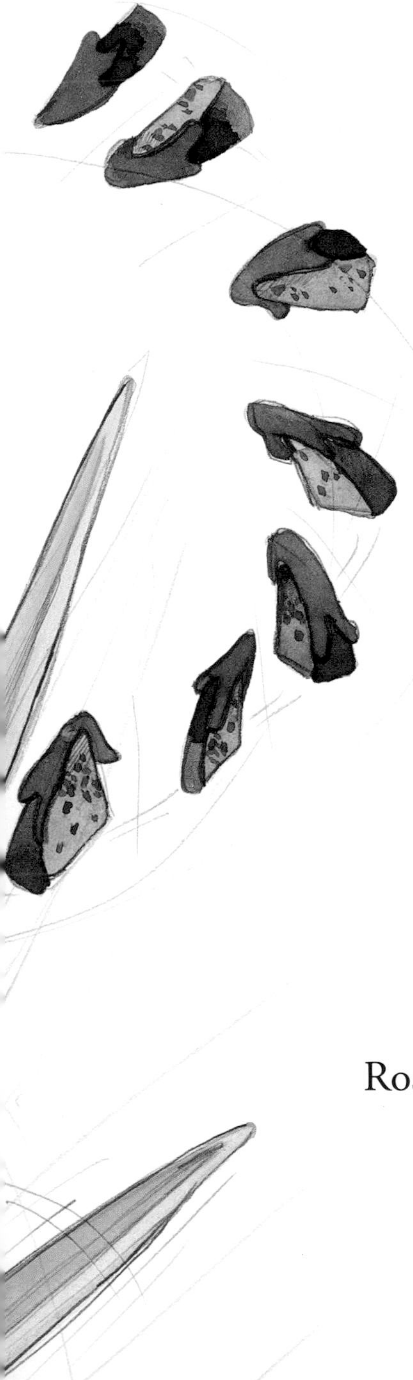

"This is really a lot of
fun," whispered Kyle to Lady
Constance behind the curtain.

"That's easy for you to
say," Constance whispered
back. "Swords, skateboards,
and chocolate cake—you don't
need a lot of practice to do your
tricks. But for me to ride the horse
standing up . . . That's a different
story."

She sighed, then bravely mounted
Rosinante and trotted out into the ring,

where she was immediately greeted with loud cheers.

Constance was a good rider, but she'd never practiced any tricks on a horse. Now she knelt on the saddle, spread her arms out as if she were about to fly, and after a few turns around the ring decided to stand up all the way. Rosinante seemed to know what the lady was trying to do and maintained a very smooth pace as Constance gradually stood up straight in the saddle. She even managed to make a curtsy!

Just as she was about to sit down again, a fly went right into Rosinante's eye. The horse whinnied and stumbled forward, and Constance lost her footing. A cry went through the crowd, as it appeared the lady was about to fall. At the last moment, however, she reached up, seized the tight-rope used for the high-wire acts, and pulled herself up while Rosinante made another round in the ring. When the horse got back to her again, Constance let go and fell safely into the saddle. It looked as if this was all part of her act.

The audience cheered wildly as the lady led her horse back behind the curtain.

"You see? I said you could do it," Kyle said with a smile, helping her down. "You're the star of the show so far, but now I have something extraspecial for the grand finale."

He turned to the audience and announced: "Ladies and gentlemen, may I ask you to step outside for our final number, where a very special attraction awaits you. Come and be amazed!"

"What are you going to do?" Nepomuk whispered to his friend.

But Kyle just winked. "You'll see."

When everyone was outside, Kyle put his fingers in his mouth and let out three shrill whistles. A few moments later two dots appeared in the sky, quickly growing larger as they approached. It was Arthur and Dragobert, and they began doing circles and loops over the heads of the spectators, flying toward—and narrowly missing—each other again and again.

"Now you'll see an air show like no one has ever seen before," Kyle cried. "Watch as the one and only Dragobert and the incredible Arthur perform their death-defying stunts!"

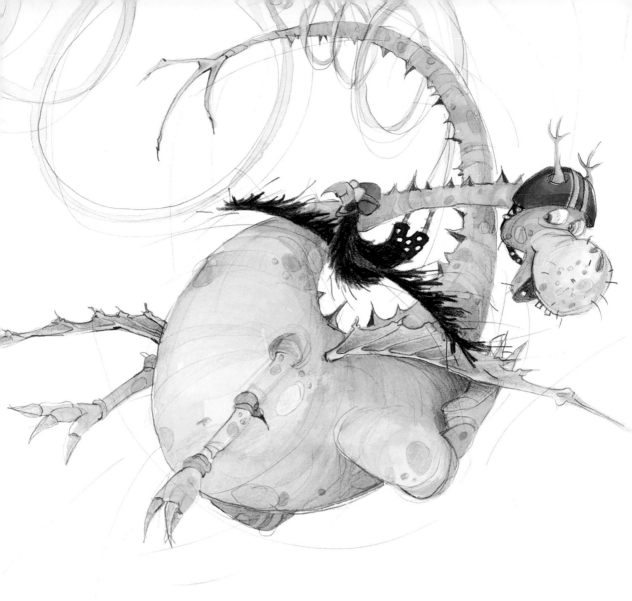

Before the performance, Kyle had asked one of the circus parrots to fetch Arthur and Dragobert so they could perform something spectacular, and they'd both put on special crash helmets to look even more daring.

The crowd stared agape at the eagle and the dragon. They'd never seen anything like this!

After a few loops, Dragobert spat out one final giant ball of fire and hissed at the audience, who drew back in awe. Arthur sat on the dragon's head, and together they went flying around town.

"Ladies and gentlemen, the performance is now over!" Kyle announced with a bow. "Kyle's Circus wants to thank you, one and all. We hope you enjoyed it."

The friends all took their places on the dragon's back and waved good-bye as the crowd broke out in cheers again. Rosinante had made friends with the two circus camels and decided to stay for a while.

A few days later Kyle received a letter from the ring-master thanking him for the fantastic performance. When the sick artists learned about Kyle's circus tricks, they laughed so hard they got better the very same day, and all the remaining performances took place as planned. For a long time after, the villagers of Waldheim spoke of the sensational circus that even had a real hissing, fire-spitting dragon and an eagle wearing crash helmets.

The Great Dumpling War

Nobody had heard from the magician Balduin for a long time, and Kyle was beginning to think he had become more civilized. In reality, Balduin was hiding deep inside his castle, plotting his revenge. After many hours pacing back and forth in his library, he'd finally come up with a devilish scheme.

"Quick, Gogol," he cried to his pet dragon. "Get me the flying kettle. We're going to settle the score with this tin man once and for all!"

Huffing and puffing, Gogol hauled the heavy copper kettle up the long, winding staircase from the kitchen in the basement to the highest part of the tower. Then the magician climbed into the giant kettle, and after a few magic words (and some thunder and lightning), the kettle lifted off and, fast as the wind, started on its journey to Fairyland East. The kettle didn't look as elegant as the flying carpet, but it did the trick.

The magician headed straight for the caves in the Troll's Teeth. His flying

121

kettle took him right to
the entrance of the largest cave,
where he landed with much clatter
and called out loudly: "Hey, trolls! Come
out. I know where we can get our hands on buckets and
buckets of chocolate."

Trolls are just wild about chocolate, and
soon there was a rumbling in the cave.
Finally, the leader of the trolls came out.
He stared down at the magician with his
quartz eyes.

"What you want?" he growled.

Balduin swallowed, then replied in a slightly trembling voice, "Uh, today is Knight Kyle's birthday, and
for his party he ordered tons and tons of chocolate. You
only have to enter the castle to get it."

That wasn't true, of course, as Kyle's birthday was
several months before. Balduin's plan was for the trolls
to attack the castle, and while everyone was
distracted, he would sneak inside

122

and steal the magic lance. He still assumed it was hidden somewhere in the cellar. The stone monsters began to groan and smack their lips as soon as they heard the word *chocolate*. One after the other, they set out for the castle, rumbling and clattering as they went.

Kyle, Prince Nepomuk, and Lady Constance were busy baking cakes and cookies in the castle's large kitchen, as they did four times a year. For each season they made a special treat: green cookies in the shape of birds for spring, yellow summer sun cookies with powdered sugar, colorful autumn leaf cookies with plum jam, and winter cookies with snowflakes made of icing. As it was now October, they were making the fall cookies, and the plum jam was already simmering on the hearth.

Just as the lady of the

castle was preparing to roll out the dough, the ground began to shake so much that the flour fell from the shelf.

"What is that?" Constance asked. "An earthquake?"

"Is it a volcano?" Nepomuk wondered. "I should probably go and make sure my wardrobe is safe."

"I suspect something worse than an earthquake or a volcano," Kyle replied. He ran to the top of the stairs in the north tower, and indeed he could see from there that the trolls were storming the castle! "*Bam-da-da, Bam-da-da, Bam!*" he heard over and over as the walls shook and tiles started falling from the roof.

Kyle pulled up

the drawbridge, but the trolls were already ramming the door with a heavy tree trunk. The water in the moat only reached up to their knees.

"Chocolate, chocolate," they kept shouting. "We want chocolate!"

Nepomuk and Constance boarded up the windows, as some of the trolls were trying to reach through the openings with their huge stone fingers.

When the attackers realized they couldn't get through the locked castle gate nor climb in through the windows, they gathered up boulders and threw them at the walls.

While this was going on, Balduin was sitting in the branches of a nearby tree, rubbing his hands gleefully. The towers were starting to teeter, and pumpkin-size pieces of the north tower were falling into the moat.

"It won't be long now," Balduin said to himself, grinning. "The walls will collapse, and I can easily get hold of the silver lance."

The friends also realized that the castle couldn't withstand the shower of stones much longer.

"What can we do?" Prince Nepomuk wailed. "We must give them chocolate, but we have only one or two bars left, and that's not enough to satisfy them."

A large rock came whizzing right over their heads and crashed through the roof of the stables, while another stone landed with a loud splash in the fountain.

"We still have a little chocolate for our cookie dough," Kyle shouted over the noise, "and a glass of chocolate cream, but—"

"The cookie dough," Constance said, interrupting him. "That's it!" She turned to her puzzled friends. "Fetch a large cooking pot and make a fire here in the courtyard," she told them.

"But . . . But why do you want to start cooking again?" asked Nepomuk. "We really have other things to worry about at the moment."

Constance disappeared into the kitchen without answering. The other two did what they were told, and soon a pot of water was bubbling over a brisk fire in the courtyard.

The walls of the castle were trembling more and more, and large cracks appeared. It wouldn't be long before the walls fell and the trolls charged inside.

Now the ramparts atop the towers came crashing down as Constance ran from the kitchen, holding a bowl of dumplings that she dropped into the boiling water.

"I threw them together from the cookie dough and filled them with plum jam," she said.

Plum dumplings? Kyle wondered. *What's she going to do with plum dumplings?*

But Constance had already left with the first batch of cooked dumplings, racing up the stairway to the south tower, where the old catapult stood. The friends hadn't tried this weapon yet against the trolls because, after all, trolls are rocks, and why should anyone shoot rocks at other rocks? Now Constance placed a plum dumpling in the bucket of the catapult and pulled the lever. With a loud whoosh, the catapult threw the dumpling at the trolls. She sent off another and another.

As the dumplings rained down on the stone monsters, they looked at them in bewilderment. Then one dumpling landed right in the mouth of the leader.

"*Mmm*, delicious," Quartzclump rumbled. "More dumplings!"

After that, the trolls didn't throw any more boulders,

but tried to catch the plum dumplings with their enormous rocky hands or in their mouths. The battle was over!

"Hey! Keep fighting!" Balduin called down from his tree. "Keep fighting I told you, you dumb rocks."

But the trolls paid no attention to him and kept catching the dumplings and swallowing them one after the other, while smacking their lips and groaning contentedly.

Constance stepped up onto the battlements and waved a white flag. "Dear trolls, instead of a fight, let's have a plum dumpling party! I can bring out wagonloads of delicious dumplings for you."

The trolls licked their lips in agreement. Then Constance put on a serious face. "Oh, but I've just heard the magician Balduin wants to eat all the dumplings himself," she said sadly. "I don't think there will be any left for you."

Slowly the trolls turned their granite heads and looked at the magician quivering in the branches of his tree. His whole plan had suddenly gone very wrong.

"You eat our dumplings?" Quartzclump rumbled like a medium-size earthquake. "You a dumpling thief?"

"Oh no, oh no," Balduin shouted. "Don't believe the lady of the castle. She's lying."

At once the trolls marched over to the magician, plucked him from the tree like a ripe pear and tossed him into the moat. He came to the surface, snorting and cursing, and swam for the shore. There he wrapped himself in his cloak and was about to run off when he slipped on a plum dumpling lying on the ground and fell—*ker-splash*— headfirst into the mush. Covered with plum jam, he hobbled off into the forest, and it was a long time before anyone heard from him again.

The friends had a wonderful autumn plum dumpling party with the trolls. And because Constance promised them they could have more dumplings whenever they wanted, the trolls all got together and rebuilt Kyle's castle finer and larger than it had ever been. Since that day, peace has reigned between the trolls and Kyle's family.

Constance's dumpling recipe was engraved in stone and displayed in the castle museum, and in his tree house on the shore of Willow Lake, Elf Aurin composed a long ballad celebrating the heroine of the Great Dumpling War.

The Ghost under the Bridge

There is one day every month that Knight Kyle doesn't like at all, and that is Cleaning Day. On that day, Lady Constance always wakes him up and shoos him out of bed very early. Then Kyle has to haul the trash down from the towers, dust off his rusty armor, and sweep behind the treasure chests. Every five minutes Constance tells him to move some piece of furniture from one corner of the room to the other.

One Cleaning Day, just as Kyle was walking down the stairs with a barrel full of trash, Prince Nepomuk came running into the courtyard. He was out of breath, and it took some time before he could speak.

"A ghost!" he was finally able to say. "Under the bridge by the old mill."

Then he hastily explained to Kyle that several travelers had reported seeing the ghost, and that it had scared them half to death. They had just barely been able to get away, and now no one dared to venture out on the road to Waldheim.

Hmm, going out to look for a ghost is way more exciting than staying here dusting and dragging trash down from the towers, Kyle mused. *Even if I really don't believe in ghosts.* "Fine," he said. "Let's go and look."

He was setting down the trash barrel when Constance appeared beside him with her feather duster.

"Here, take this," she said. "In the library there are five hundred and ninety-three books that still need dusting, and you didn't pick up your swords in the living room, and there are cobwebs in the armory, and—"

"Unfortunately, I can't now," he said, interrupting her. "A knight's duty calls! A ghost has been seen on the road to Waldheim, and I must chase it away. See you later!"

Constance stood there with the feather duster, too surprised even to protest, as he hurried off with Nepomuk.

Around noon they were approaching the bridge not far from the old mill.

"It is said the ghost used to live in the mill," Nepomuk whispered. "But because no one ventures there anymore, he has gone to live under the bridge where it's easier for him to scare people."

"Then let's go and see if people can scare a ghost, too," Kyle replied with a grin. He took out two bedsheets from his pack.

With his sword he made two slits in each sheet for eyeholes and handed one to his friend. "Here, put this on," he said.

"When Constance finds out about these sheets," Nepomuk said, "she's not going to be happy!"

"Well, you've got to make some sacrifices if you want

to chase ghosts," Kyle replied. He'd already pulled a bed-sheet over his head and was creeping toward the bridge. Nepomuk followed cautiously.

When they'd almost reached the river, there was a sudden screech from under the bridge, like fingernails on a blackboard. "*Eeeek!*" Then "*Uhuuuu!*" followed by a hoarse cackle. After a while a loud voice told them, "Drop everything and flee . . . while you still can . . . Shoo!"

"The ghost," Nepomuk gasped, feeling rather queasy now.

"Let's wait and see," Kyle whispered.

They crept closer and could now see something white crouching under the bridge. It really was a ghost! It was wearing a sheet just like the two friends, but this sheet was already quite dirty and had many holes, and through one of those holes they could see the brim of a red hat.

"Aha," said Kyle. "I think I know who our ghost is." Then, in a forceful voice he demanded, "What

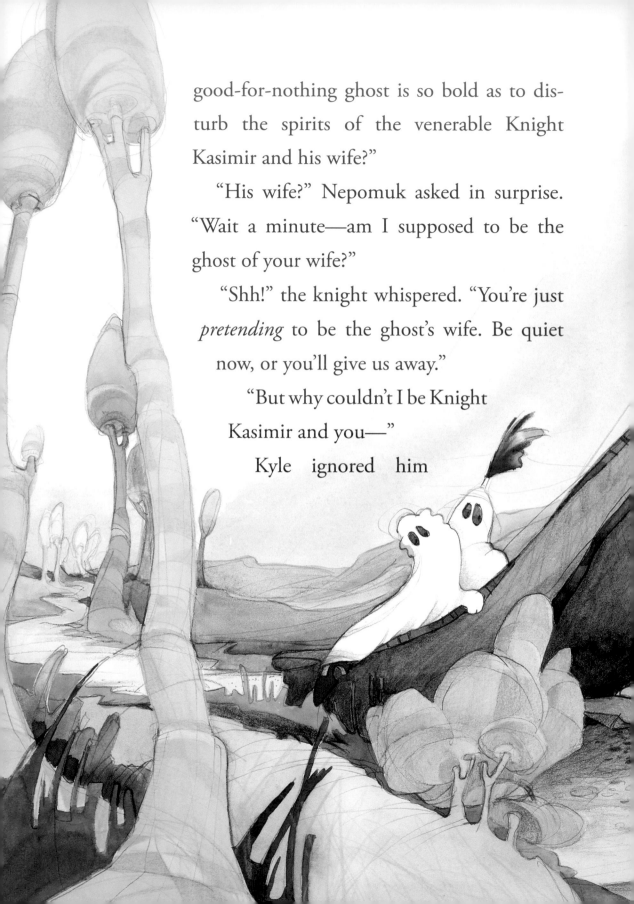

good-for-nothing ghost is so bold as to disturb the spirits of the venerable Knight
Kasimir and his wife?"

"His wife?" Nepomuk asked in surprise.
"Wait a minute—am I supposed to be the
ghost of your wife?"

"Shh!" the knight whispered. "You're just
pretending to be the ghost's wife. Be quiet
now, or you'll give us away."

"But why couldn't I be Knight
Kasimir and you—"

Kyle   ignored   him

and continued. "Since olden times the two of us, ghosts of Kasimir and Kunigunde, have been wandering through the enchanted forest, and no one has ever challenged us. Our vengeance will be swift and sure!"

In fact, there was an old legend that said Kyle's great-grandparents Kasimir and Kunigunde would sometimes wander through the forests and lie in wait for evil poachers. Now the ghost under the bridge was frightened.

"Uh, venerable Kasimir, I didn't mean to offend you," the ghost said in a trembling voice. "I'm very, very sorry."

"Too late!" Kyle boomed and raised his arms so it appeared Kasimir's ghost was slowly rising up.

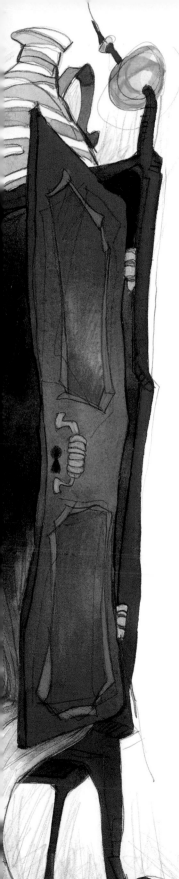

"*Eeek!*" cried the ghost with the sheet full of holes. "Help! Two real ghosts!"

He ran out from under the bridge and into the old mill, slamming the door behind him.

"Come on, we'll go and get this cowardly ghost!" Kyle shouted. He and the prince ran to the mill and entered the dark, dusty room on the ground floor. It did look pretty spooky here. A few smashed crates lay on the floor, and in the dim light they could just make out a rickety stairway leading to the floor above. Mice were squeaking and scurrying around.

"Where might our ghost be hiding?" Nepomuk whispered. "He couldn't have made himself invisible, like Balduin with his magic helmet, could he?"

Kyle was about to reply when he

139

noticed an old wardrobe closet with one of its doors ajar. Through the small crack he could see the corner of a dirty old sheet. The two friends winked at each other, then crept over to the closet and whispered, "One, two, three" and tore open the door. Cowering inside was the most pathetic ghost anyone could imagine.

"Please, please, don't hurt me!" he wailed. "I will never again disturb the tranquility of your eternal rest."

"Only if you show us who you really are," replied Kyle, who, like Nepomuk, was still wearing his bedsheet.

The ghost removed his own shabby sheet, and from under it emerged the robber Rasputin, whom Kyle had already recognized by his red hat as he hid under the bridge. Rasputin was trembling like a leaf.

"May I, uh . . . May I leave now?" he whined.

"Ah, it's not as easy as that," said Nepomuk in a high-pitched falsetto, remembering he was supposed to be the ghost of Kunigunde. "First you will tell us what the point of this masquerade is."

The robber confessed he'd dressed as a ghost in order to rob travelers on the road. When they saw him dressed in a sheet, they ran away screaming—even faster than usual—and then he could easily steal all the things they'd left behind.

"I . . . I'll never, never do this again," he promised.

"That's not enough," Kyle said, spreading out his arms. "I, the ghost of the Knight Kasimir, order you to clean my entire castle today as punishment. Swear to me that you will, on your robber's honor, or we will carry you off with us to the Otherworld."

"I swear, I swear!" wailed the robber, who only wanted this nightmare to stop. "Believe me, I didn't know there were real ghosts here in the forest."

"Oh, there aren't really," replied Kyle, pulling the bedsheet off his head. Nepomuk now also showed his face.

The robber was so astounded his eyes almost popped out of his head. "You tricked me!" he yelled.

"Just like you tricked the travelers," Nepomuk said.

"Remember your promise. You gave your robber's word of honor." Then he added with a wink: "Who knows, maybe Kasimir's ghost does exist, and if so, he's definitely mad at you, and only Kyle, as his descendant, can calm him down."

Grumbling, Rasputin accompanied the two friends to Kyle's castle, where Constance was anxiously awaiting them.

"Ah, here you are at last!" she said. "I was beginning to wonder if Kyle was abandoning his cleaning duties."

Kyle shook his head with annoyance. "How can you even think that?" he said, then pointed at Rasputin. "I even brought someone along who can help us."

Constance was both astonished and pleased.

And so the robber spent the entire afternoon cleaning, sweeping, and dusting the castle. And whenever it seemed he was about to quit and run away, Kyle reminded him of his promise—and of the ghost of Kasimir, which just might be floating through the halls, watching him.

Finally, in the evening, Rasputin had to wash the

three ghost shrouds while Kyle, Nepomuk, and
Constance sat around a crackling fire, telling all
the ghost stories they'd heard about Kasimir
and Kunigunde.

A Giant Problem

One sunny day in autumn after almost all the leaves had fallen from the trees, Knight Kyle had nothing at all to do for once and was terribly bored. They had cleaned up the kitchen and the cellar, finished baking the fall cookies, and brushed and fed Rosinante. Kyle had even swept away the cobwebs in the castle towers.

Kyle sat in the courtyard glumly, not knowing what to do on such a beautiful day. Just as he was going to let out another loud yawn, Lady Constance came in skipping and singing. She had strung herself a necklace of chestnuts, and her freshly combed hair shone like yellow leaves in the autumn sun.

"We could go on a picnic," she said cheerfully, "and you can help me

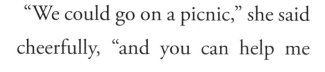

with my leaf collection. I need to find a few more maple and beech leaves. Would you like to help?"

At first, Kyle pretended to be a bit unsure, not wanting to show how pleased he was that Constance had asked him and not Prince Nepomuk. Both of them were, as we know, a bit in love with the lady of the castle.

"Why not?" he said after a while. "It would feel good to get out and stretch my legs."

They packed a basket with cheese, raspberry soda, bread, and apple cake, then they strolled together through the forest, throwing leaves at each other and looking for shiny chestnuts to make chains, crowns, and other figures when they got back to the castle.

After walking about a mile, they reached Willow Lake and sat down to rest under an oak tree along the shore. Kyle's mouth watered at the thought of all the delicious

things in their picnic basket. As he was about to bite into a large piece of cake, the earth began to rumble. It

shook so hard that the cake
fell out of his hand, and
his cup of soda tipped over.
Kyle couldn't help thinking
of the time not long ago when the
trolls attacked his castle. Or was this a real earthquake?

"Kyle, what's happening?" Constance shouted. "I didn't think our fall picnic would turn out like this!"

146

The shaking became stronger and stronger, the oak trees above them swayed back and forth, ripples formed in the lake, and waves splashed against the shore.

Just then Kyle saw a huge figure stomping through the forest, heading toward them. It was a giant from the other side of Dragon Mountain, apparently just passing through. His shaggy head stood out like a clump of moss above the tops of the tallest trees; his beard got caught on the branches, ripping them off as he passed; and wherever he stepped, the trees fell to both sides like toothpicks.

Finally, the giant arrived at Willow Lake. "Ah, a bath!" he grunted. "Just what I need!" With a sigh of relief, he slipped into the lake.

Water overflowed the shore, swamping a few small trees, while the giant sat there in Willow Lake as if he were in a bathtub, washing his face with his massive hands.

"Ah, good," he grumbled, then took such a big drink of water that the terrified fish jumped away.

"Hey, you there," Constance called out. She and Kyle had climbed up into a nearby oak to get a better look. Since Constance knew by now it was no earthquake, she had gotten back some of her courage.

"Hey, you scoundrel," she cried again. "Here we are!"

The giant turned toward her, squinting a bit so he could see the little lady and the equally tiny knight on the branch, and suddenly he appeared worried.

"Oh, I'm sorry," he said. "Did I scare you?"

"You're asking if you scared us?" Constance gasped. "Just look around. There's hardly a tree left standing, and all the animals for miles around have run away. You made a *giant* mess!" She pointed at the shoreline; in certain places only the tops of some birch trees rose above the water.

Now they heard another angry outburst that got

louder and louder. It was Elf Aurin, rowing across the lake toward them in his boat made of reeds.

"A wave almost knocked over my beautiful tree house!" he shouted. "And my whole audience ran away: the mole, the marten, even the worm . . . And that was after I'd performed an especially beautiful song for them on my harp. It didn't even put them to sleep!"

"I'm terribly sorry," the giant grumbled. "Everyone is always afraid of me because I'm so large. I only wish I were as small as you. Then I'd surely have more friends." A tear glistened in the giant's left eye, rolled down his cheek, and landed in the lake with a splash.

"We're so sorry, too," Constance said now in a softer voice so as not to frighten the giant. She felt very sorry she'd scolded him so much.

Kyle thought it over. "Hmm, we can ask Fairy Laureana," he said. "Maybe she knows a spell that will make you smaller." He had already given Laureana the shrinking potion he'd found in his great-grandfather's chest, but there wasn't enough of it to shrink a giant.

"Do you think so?" the giant asked, already looking a bit happier.

"In any case we can try," Constance replied. "There's no one who knows more about magic potions than Fairy Laureana."

"If anyone can help you, it's her," agreed Elf Aurin, who was already not so angry anymore. After all, it wasn't the giant's fault that he was large, anymore than it was Aurin's fault that he was small.

Together they started out, with the giant carefully putting one foot in front of the other so he wouldn't knock down any more trees.

When they arrived at the fairy's cabin, the giant was about to knock, but Kyle waved him off.

"Don't touch anything," he warned. "You'll just break it! Anyway, I'm sure she heard your footsteps already."

The giant lay down sadly in the clearing and sighed. When Fairy Laureana saw her new patient and heard about his problem, she shrugged.

"A difficult case," she said. "But I'll see what I can do."

Laureana started collecting elderberries, buttercups, and dwarf greens in the forest and made a large kettle of soup from them. Then she hectically leafed through her book of magic, shaking her head.

"What's the matter?" Kyle asked.

"Something is still missing," Laureana muttered, "something very important, namely a mountain violet. It only grows on the highest peaks of Dragon Mountain."

"We probably can't ask Dragobert to help us with that," mused Aurin. "With his huge claws he might crush such a tender little plant."

"How about Arthur the eagle?" Constance asked. "If we give him a few of my fall cookies, maybe he'll go and get us a mountain violet."

Everyone agreed that was a good idea! Constance put her fingers in her mouth and whistled, and soon

151

Arthur appeared overhead. When he heard their plan, he preened his wings nervously.

"*Caw*—I don't know," he croaked. "On the highest peaks of Dragon Mountain it's as cold as the moon. Anyway, up there—*caw*—I'll hardly have any air to breathe."

"You just have to do it," Constance pleaded. "The poor giant needs your help."

"*Caw*—well, okay then." Arthur spread his wings. "Who knows, if I don't do it, this clumsy giant might someday trample my nest. *Caw, caw, caw.*"

He fluttered away, and soon the friends—and even the giant—were just little specks the size of ants in the colorful autumn forest. As Arthur climbed higher and higher, icy winds almost blew him into steep cliffs more than once, and he could feel the air getting thinner. It was so cold his blood almost began to freeze, and his wings beat slower. He wouldn't be able to stand it up there much longer.

Arthur gazed over the snow-white summits, but nowhere could he spot a mountain violet. Shards of ice formed on his wings, making them heavier and heavier, and just as he felt he couldn't go on, he saw a flash of blue on a distant mountain peak. With his last bit of strength, he flew toward it, and indeed it was a mountain violet, blue and radiant like a star in the white landscape.

Gently Arthur took the mountain violet in his claws, then plunged downward, and not until the air became warmer again did he spread his wings and soar toward Fairyland Forest.

"He has the violet! He has it!" the friends cried as they saw Arthur glide down into the clearing, clutching the flower. "Three cheers for our brave eagle!"

Arthur collapsed in a pile of leaves as the last bits of ice on his wings melted, then he fell into a deep sleep.

Now Laureana got to work, plucking the petals from the stems of the violets, rubbing them in her hands, and

sprinkling the powder into the bubbling potion. There was a tinkling sound,
as if somewhere a little bell was being rung,
and now a delicate aroma like a whole field of
strawberries filled the air. The giant's potion
was ready!

"Here you go," Laureana said to him as she
pointed to the heavy kettle. "Be sure to drink
it all."

The giant lifted the kettle, which to him
seemed as small as a cup for a doll, and put
it to his lips. He slurped the steaming potion,
then sat down again, being especially careful not to

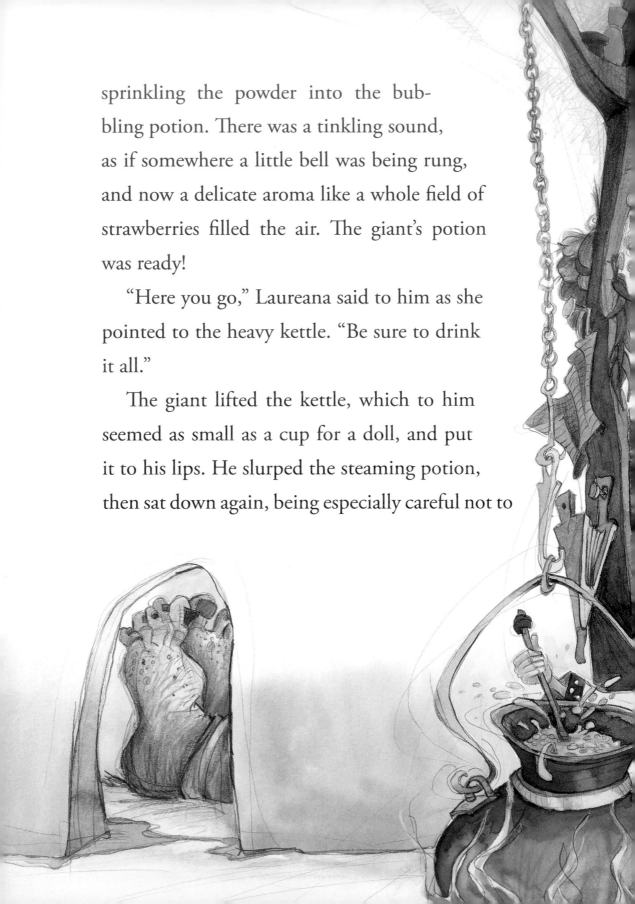

crush Laureana's little house. They all waited, staring at him.

After a while Kyle whispered: "He looks just as large as before."

"Maybe the potion isn't working," Constance murmured.

"Maybe I should sing a song," said Aurin. "For example, I could—"

At that very moment the giant began to shrink—first he was as tall as the trees, then as big as the fairy's cabin, and then, no taller than Kyle, or maybe a bit smaller. He didn't stop shrinking until he was the size of a child.

The tiny giant hopped around in a circle like a little bearded garden gnome.

"I'm small. I'm small," he cheered. His voice, which used to be so loud, was now so soft you could hardly hear it. "Nobody will be afraid of me anymore!"

That was true. No one had to be afraid of this giant anymore.

The little man thanked them all effusively, especially Fairy Laureana and Arthur the eagle, who had awakened and was wrapped in a woolen shawl. Then the tiny giant waved to them, went on his way, and had soon disappeared among the trees.

Later Kyle heard that the enchanted giant had appeared at carnivals and earned a lot of money. He now called himself Benjamin, the world's smallest giant, and people paid lots of gold coins to see a giant they didn't have to be afraid of.

Fire and Ice

On a frosty winter morning, Kyle was having a wonderful dream, in which he had finally found the lost silver lance. He was galloping on Rosinante through clouds of pink cotton candy, toward the sun, when suddenly—

"Kyle! Kyle, wake up!" Constance cried. "Hurry up, you sleepyhead! Look! It finally snowed."

Kyle shook himself awake and ran to the window. Snowflakes were falling from the sky like cotton balls, and many trees were already covered in white.

"Come on, let's go sledding," Lady Constance pleaded.

Kyle agreed enthusiastically. Ever since they'd brought Dragobert down from Dragon Mountain on a big sled when he was injured, Kyle had been working

on his turbo-charged racing sled. The only thing missing was the snow. He gulped down his morning cocoa and a roll with jelly, then ran outside with Constance.

Overnight it had gotten bitterly cold. Prince Nepomuk was already waiting impatiently in front of the castle gate with his sled, and together they walked to the big sledding hill in the forest where they held their races every year.

"I'm going to win this time!" Nepomuk boasted. "I've

160

greased my runners with royal hair wax, so no one will be able to beat me."

"Don't be so sure!" said Kyle. "I've carved my sled from the wood of the quick-fir, and it takes off like Rosinante when he gets stung by a wasp."

They bickered awhile about who was the fastest sledder in Fairyland East while Constance took her sled, pulled it up the hill, and went whizzing by them so close they were splattered with snow. They were left standing there like two snowmen.

"While you were quarreling, I've won ten times already!" Constance shouted.

The two stopped arguing, and the three friends raced down the hill many times, with different winners. They had the most fun when they tied all three sleds together and zoomed down the hill like a train that had gone off the rails.

They were just starting to build a really high ski jump

when Constance cried out: "Look at that! Is it the sun or the moon, or maybe even a new star?"

The heavy snow clouds overhead were glowing reddish-orange, and a few moments later the friends saw a fiery ball that got bigger and bigger. The air became so warm that the snow around them began to melt.

"I think it's a meteor!" Kyle said excitedly. "I've read about them—take cover!"

Terrified, they jumped into the slushy snow, and in the next moment the bright object whooshed past overhead. There was a bang, then silence, and off in the distance they saw a huge cloud of smoke rising from the forest. They could smell fire and sulfur in the air.

"That was close," Nepomuk gasped, knocking the snow from his royal jacket. "If that meteor had hit the castle, it would have left nothing but a big hole."

"The fairy's house!" Constance exclaimed. "It's somewhere over there. I hope nothing happened to Fairy Laureana."

They hurried through the woods as the frightened animals came running toward them.

"It's the end of the world! The end of the world!" cried a very scared rabbit hopping past them. A flock of startled crows flew by, cawing furiously; squeaking mice scurried between Constance's legs, which she did not like at all; and a nervous mother fox kept calling for her cub.

"Fabian!" she yelled. "Fabian, where are you?"

"Don't worry, your son will show up soon," said Kyle, trying to reassure her. "He probably just ran away with the others."

But the mother fox shook her head. "He's always so curious about things. He probably ran to get a better look at that shining thing lying over there in the forest. Oh, I hope nothing happened to him!"

"We'll go over right away and check," Kyle told her.

The friends hurried off and discovered to their relief that the meteor hadn't fallen on the fairy's house, but in a deserted part of the forest. As they got closer, they discovered more and more fallen, burned trees. More frightened animals came running toward them, but fortunately none of them had been badly hurt.

Finally, they came to a clearing, and in the middle was a gigantic crater, hissing and smoking. It smelled so strongly of rotten eggs that Constance held her nose in disgust.

"We were really lucky," Nepomuk said. "Here, at least, it can't do any harm. We can tell the animals that they're safe."

At that very moment, they heard a soft whimpering that seemed to come directly from the crater. They approached cautiously, and far below, amid the clouds of smoke, they saw a reddish glow. A charred root reached down into the middle of the crater with a little fox cub clinging to it and wailing desperately.

"That must be Fabian, the runaway fox," said Kyle. "We have to help him before he falls into the pit!"

He took the rope they had used earlier to tie their sleds together, wrapped it around a tree, and slowly lowered himself into the hole. He was soon sweating profusely inside his armor. The little fox watched him wide-eyed, still clinging to the root as the fire singed his furry tail.

"I'll be there in just a second," Kyle promised as the crater continued to smoke and hiss. Now the knight could see the meteorite, as large as a soccer net and glowing like coal. The odor of rotten eggs was even more unpleasant than before.

Kyle had grown somewhat accustomed to the heat, however, and was able to let himself down the final few yards to the cub. He was dangling directly over Fabian, but his hands were so sweaty, he had trouble holding on to the rope and nearly slipped a few times. Then he remembered the iron gloves he always kept on his belt. He carefully put them on. Now he had a good grip!

"I've got you!" Kyle said, holding the whimpering bundle of fur by the neck.

He signaled Nepomuk and Constance to pull them up. At the edge of the crater the anxious mother fox didn't know whether to scold her little cub or lick him all over with joy.

Constance, still trembling all over, rubbed her hands together. "Now let's tell all the animals in the forest they don't have to be afraid anymore, and then we can go home. It's awfully cold here," she said, her teeth chattering.

"I don't feel cold at all," replied Kyle with a grin. "It's nice and warm down there. It almost feels like you're in a bathtub . . ."

Suddenly he beamed from ear to ear as he always did when he had a good idea.

"Of course!" he cried. "I know how to convince the animals not to be afraid of the meteorite."

"How are you going to do that?" Nepomuk asked.

"You'll see," Kyle said. "First, you need to get your bathing suit."

"But it's winter!" Constance and Nepomuk said at the same time.

Kyle just smiled.

The very same day, the knight had the diamond dwarfs build him an iron tub just the right size to fit into the steaming crater. When the tub was

167

filled with water, they all had a wonderfully warm swimming pool. Every time Kyle and his friends were finished sledding, they stopped to splash around in the water. The animals gathered around for warmth, and some even joined in. Fabian was the best swimmer of all. The meteorite remained red-hot for many weeks, and even in the most bitter cold everyone now had a place that was always cozy and warm.

And if anyone complained that it smelled of rotten eggs, Constance had some good advice—just hold your nose and jump in!

A New Year

The year was coming to an end, and all of Fairyland East was eagerly looking forward to New Year's Eve.

Every New Year's Eve there was a fireworks display at Kyle's castle, and everyone was invited: the knights Max, Bertram, and Oswald; Elf Aurin; Dragobert; Arthur the eagle; and Fairy Laureana, who had been busy at work for the last few weeks building her famous New Year's rockets. Laureana's fireworks lit up the night sky as if by magic in all the colors of the rainbow, with figures of castles and dragons, grazing deer, roaring lions, and brilliant birds of paradise.

All the animals in the forest had received invitations, too. The guests of honor this year were the old raccoon who had warned Laureana about the robber Rasputin

and the family of foxes whose youngest member had recently been saved from the crater by Kyle. Kyle had even considered inviting the trolls, but that would have been too dangerous, since their singing and dancing could knock down a house—and had done just that on a few occasions.

The only ones nobody wanted at the party were the evil magician Balduin and Rasputin. That really angered the two of them, of course, and high up in Balduin's storm-tossed castle they gloomily plotted their revenge.

"Kyle will soon find out what happens when he doesn't invite me, the great Balduin!" the magician snarled. "Someday when I rule over the whole land, I won't invite him to my party, either. In fact, every year I'll *disinvite* him. Oh ho! Instead of getting an invitation to come, he'll get an order to stay away. See how he likes that!"

"But first, you'll have to get your hands on the magic silver lance," Rasputin reminded him, "because only the person who possesses the lance can rule the land—that's an ancient law."

"You blockhead! Of course I know that," Balduin said. "And don't you think I'll do everything in my power to get hold of it? But I need a surefire plan."

He walked back and forth, fuming. Then he stopped and snapped his fingers.

"Of course! The fireworks!" he exclaimed. "Maybe we're not invited, but we can still ruin all their fun and get the lance at the same time."

Balduin's plan was to enter the castle secretly and set off all the rockets at once. In the confusion he would search the castle for the silver lance, steal it, and run away again. Simple, right?

The two villains put on their winter coats, climbed aboard the flying kettle, and sped straight down to the forest. Since all the animals had been invited to the party, none of them noticed the two sneaky sneaks sneaking through the dark forest toward the castle. There, Rasputin threw a rope ladder over the wall and helped the clumsy magician climb over.

The party was in full swing. The frogs, the finches, and the crickets sang the special New Year's music while a bear plucked a double bass and a wild boar beat the drums, and the guests merrily danced the Fairyland polka. Lady Constance danced with both Kyle and Nepomuk so neither would be disappointed. On each table stood a large bubbling bowl of chocolate fondue along with the last wrinkled autumn apples and some strange prickly pink fruit that Knight Max had brought back with him from his last voyage.

None of the guests noticed Balduin or Rasputin creeping toward the shed out back where the fireworks were stored.

"Hah! When we set them all off, there will be such a racket that no one will notice anything but the ringing in their ears." Balduin giggled.

"Isn't it dangerous?" the robber asked.

Balduin waved him off. "Oh, that's no problem. We just have to take cover in time."

The villains looked around the dark shed and discovered a crate with a note scrawled on it:

Caution! Fireworks! Keep away from flame!

When the two opened the crate, they stared in awe at the New Year's Eve fireworks. There were small ones and large ones; red, yellow, green, and blue ones. Some had a bird on the tip, others a dragon's head, and all of them had a long fuse at the end.

"Oh, how beautiful!" murmured the robber. "I always wanted to have rockets like these."

Balduin gathered up some dry straw from the floor, then turned impatiently to Rasputin.

"Now give me the matches," he said, "so I can light the straw and throw it in the box."

"But I still think it's very dangerous," the robber replied anxiously. "My old robber grandmother always told me not to play with fire—and certainly not with fireworks."

"You can hide over there behind those old barrels, you scaredy-cat," Balduin said, pointing to a far corner. "But hurry up and give me the matches." He was trembling with anticipation. "Today I'll finally get my hands on the silver lance. I can feel it in my bones!"

He took the matches from Rasputin, and soon the dry bundle of straw was burning brightly in his hands.

"Ouch!" the magician cried and threw the bundle into the crate.

For a few moments nothing happened, and Balduin was beginning to wonder if the fire had gone out. But then, there was a hissing, whirring, humming, and whistling in the box, and Rasputin fled behind a barrel while the magician stared spellbound at the crate, from which a stinking black cloud of smoke was rising.

"This is surely my most evil plan so far," Balduin whispered. "Truly worthy of a great magician. Soon Kyle will have to bow down to me at last and—"

That was as far as he got, because at that moment the crate exploded into a million pieces. Rockets shot in all directions, many of them right through the rotted roof of the shed and up into the night sky; some veered to the right, some to the left, and some crashed straight down again into the ground, where they blew apart. The stench of pitch and sulfur was everywhere.

When Balduin tried to flee behind a barrel, too, an

especially large rocket with a dragon's head flew under the magician's cape and got stuck there.

"Hey, hey . . . that tickles. Ouch, it burns—" was all Balduin could say before the rocket carried him off. His head banged into some bricks, then he went straight up through the roof of the shed into the starry sky, where the other rockets were already hissing and exploding.

"Help!" Balduin shouted. "I'm flying to the moon!"

The party guests stopped dancing and watched the fireworks exploding above them.

"Did Fairy Laureana begin early this year?" Kyle wondered. "It's not midnight yet."

But then he saw the screaming magician loop over their heads and shoot up again like an arrow. Balduin was lucky, though, as his rocket did not explode; it just zoomed merrily to the left, to the right, up, and down, until it got snagged with its squirming passenger on the

flagpole of the north tower.

Balduin dangled there, spinning around and around like a weather vane.

"Get me down!" he howled.

"Please," he added.

"I told him it was dangerous to play with fire," whispered the robber, who had come out of the shed now that it seemed safe. In the darkness, no one recognized him.

"Help!" Balduin cried again. "I'm afraid of heights. I'm getting sick."

"Our new weather vane is a little too loud for me." Kyle laughed. "I guess I'll just have to help him down."

He ran up the stairs to the tower room and climbed through a trapdoor to the roof. But when he saw the trembling magician hanging from the flagpole, he suddenly stopped.

"Wait, I recognize this flagpole," he muttered. "It's the—"

"It's the magic silver lance! I'm hanging from the magic silver lance!" shrieked Balduin, who had realized it at the same moment.

Kyle shook his head in amazement. Evidently his bumbling great-grandfather Kasimir had simply used the lance as a flagpole, and for all these years it had been standing right there on the roof before Kyle's very eyes. And until now, no one had noticed.

"The silver lance," he called down to his friends. "It's here! We've finally found it."

"The magician said he'd be holding it in his hands before the day was over," said the robber Rasputin, who had been watching it all from down below. "Well, he was right. He's actually holding it in his hands. Or rather, it's holding him. Hmm . . . But not for much longer, it seems."

The robber was right, for at that very moment, the magician's cloak tore apart with an ugly ripping sound, and Balduin fell screaming from the tower roof into a huge snow pile, where he remained, exhausted.

The magician was so shaken by his terrifying trip that

the animals took pity on him and revived him with a few spoonfuls of chocolate fondue. In the meantime, the shamefaced robber had revealed his true identity, too, and was dunking his piece of apple cake into the chocolate sauce.

"You ruined our New Year's fireworks," Constance said, scolding them. "They weren't supposed to go off until midnight."

"But only because you didn't invite us to the celebration," the robber grumbled. "We weren't even invited to Kyle's birthday party."

"But the only reason I didn't invite you was because you two are always so mean to us," explained Kyle, who had taken the slower route down the tower stairs. For now, he had left the lance on the roof, which seemed the safest spot, with the magician and the robber around.

"Maybe I was a bit mean to you and stole the chocolate egg," Rasputin said, "but only *after* you didn't invite me to the party. If I'd had an invitation—"

"Oh, and how about the magic book you stole from

Fairy Laureana?" Prince Nepomuk said, joining in. "And the time Balduin promised chocolate to the trolls if they attacked Kyle's castle?"

"That wasn't my fault. That was—"

"Oh, stop!" Constance interrupted. "Just stop right now. These arguments are more deafening than the fireworks."

The bell in the castle announced the hour of midnight.

"Listen, I have a suggestion," the lady said, addressing the crowd, including the many curious animals that had drawn near. "The old year is past and a new one has begun. Let's put aside the old arguments and celebrate New Year's together. Three cheers for Fairyland East! It's a big enough place that we can all live here together in peace. Hip, hip, hooray!"

"Hip, hip, hooray!" they responded, and even the robber Rasputin joined in. The animals applauded with their paws, claws, and feathers.

Still lying on a pile of slushy snow, the magician Balduin was about to start quarreling again when Constance stepped up to him and gave him a kiss on the cheek. He remained silent, and later, when no one was watching, he even smiled, a bit ashamed of himself.

The guests celebrated into the early-morning hours. Fortunately, some of the rockets were spared in the big explosion, and now to the accompaniment of much cheering, they were fired into the sky, where they exploded and burst into many shapes and colors.

From that day on, the magic silver lance was accorded

a place of honor in the castle museum along with Constance's famous dumpling recipe, Balduin's helmet of invisibility, and Dragobert's gold-plated tooth. Until one day . . . yes, it really did disappear.

But that's another story.

Thanks

A big thanks to the former class 3b in the Camerloher Elementary School in Munich, whose enthusiasm encouraged me to write this book. Without your imagination and enjoyment of these tales, Kyle and the entire Fairyland East would not exist. Remain childlike, as long as you live!

About the Author

Photo © Gerald Von Foris

Oliver Pötzsch spent years working for Bavarian Broadcasting and now devotes his time entirely to writing. He lives in Munich. His adult historical novels made him internationally famous. *Knight Kyle and the Magic Silver Lance* is his first book for children.

About the Translator

Lee Chadeayne is a former classical musician, college lecturer, and owner of a language translation company in Massachusetts. He is a charter member of the American Literary Translators Association (ALTA) and a Life Member of the American Translators Association (ATA), and he has served as editor of both the ALTA newsletter and the ATA Chronicle.

His translated works focus on music, art, language, history, and general literature; notable works include

The Wandering Harlot and The Lady of the Castle by Iny Lorentz; Synagogue and Church in the Middle Ages by Wolfgang Seiferth; Once Upon a Time: On the Nature of Fairy Tales by Max Lüthi; and the bestselling Hangman's Daughter series of five historical novels (to date) by Oliver Pötzsch.

Details at chadeayne.net/books

About the Illustrator

Sibylle Hammer lives and works as a freelance illustrator and graphic designer in Munich.

She is employed full-time for the *Bayerische Rundfunk* (Bavarian Radio and Television) as a designer, illustrator, TV set designer, and as an animator for educational television.

Ever since her childhood years in the Munich area, she has had a passion for drawing and painting.

In addition to her work for the Bavarian Radio and

TV, she writes and designs children's books for various publishers.

For years, Sibylle Hammer has worked for *edition bilibri,* a publisher of multilingual books. Her best-known book to date is *Arthur and Anton* (2005)

She was awarded a prize for the best school book of 2003 (published by the Cornelsen-Verlag).

Oliver Pötzsch und Sibylle Hammer have enjoyed working together often since they were employed by the *Bayerische Rundfunk.*